The Chorus Chronicles

by Alejandro Canelos

The Chorus Chronicles
by Alejandro Canelos
Published by Neotenic Press
© 2026 Alejandro N. Canelos
All rights reserved. No portion of this book may be reproduced in any form without permission from the publisher, except as permitted by U.S. copyright law.
Cover art and book design by Pia Zaverukha
Edited by Rebecca Salome
ISBN: 979-8-9856789-9-4 (paperback)

www.alejandrocanelos.com

Also by Alejandro Canelos

The Neotenic Queen: Tales of Sex and Survival in the Sonoran Desert

Hunters and Thieves and Other Stories

Ten-Minute Dramas for the Stage

Hopscotch to Infinity: Short Plays for Kids to Read and Perform

Short Fiction for Alcoholics

Program

Catalog of Singers 1

The Repertory Singers, Part I *Dr. Armand Tilton*
  Music Director

  The Retreat 5
  The Audition 13
  Too Many Takes 23
  I Know That Brand 31
  The Solfege Olympiad 39
  Not Forgotten 51
  Once in a Lullaby 59
  The Gibson 69
  Twelve Lines 81
  Symptomatic 89

Intermission: The Symphony Chorus *Dr. Sophia Dahl*
  Chorus Director

  The Verdi Disaster 101
  Howard and the Maestro 109
  Denied 121

THE REPERTORY SINGERS, PART II   *Dr. Diana Simoneaux*
                                              Music Director

    Metronome Mutiny..133

    An Alto in Need..141

    The App...149

    Soprano Bond..161

    A New Tenor..169

    Choraliers...179

    The Void...189

    Four Sopranos and an Elevator......................................197

    A Betrayal..207

ENCORE   *Emma and Theo*

    Saved for Last...219

Repertory Singers

Christina	Alto
Daniel	Tenor, board president
David	Bass, section leader
Eleanor	Soprano, section leader
Elroy	Tenor, section leader
Georgia	Alto, section leader
Gretchen	Soprano
Hal	Bass
Hazel	Soprano
Janey	Tenor
Judith	Soprano
Katie	Soprano
Marnie	Soprano
Mary Pat	Alto
Philip	Bass
Rochelle	Soprano
Samuel	Bass
Susannah	Soprano
Theo	Bass
Velma	Soprano
Will	Tenor
Xavier	Tenor

Symphony Chorus

Chelsea	Alto
Esau	Tenor
Howard	Tenor
Keegan	Bass, chorus manager
Lizzie	Soprano
Matilda	Alto
Ted	Tenor
Victor	Tenor

The Repertory Singers

Part I

Dr. Armand Tilton, Music Director

The Retreat

The all-day retreat kicking off the Repertory Singers' thirty-fourth season was held at the home of basses David and Hal. The venue had been chosen five years running because of its expansive living room, wraparound patio, and plentiful spaces for small groups. Present were thirty-nine of forty-five singers, as well as their music director of twenty-seven years, Dr. Armand Tilton, and accompanist Jackie.

Seated in a circle in Hal's home office—or study, as he liked to call it—were Dr. Tilton, Jackie, soprano section leader Eleanor, alto Mary Pat, tenor Janey, and basses Theo and Samuel.

Theo said, "We get the director *and* the accompanist. Does that make us lucky or unlucky?" He laughed.

Eleanor said, "I say lucky. Most directors wouldn't stoop to joining a breakout session."

Dr. Tilton said, "And most accompanists don't show up to retreats. So thank you, Jackie, for participating."

"I didn't have any gigs today," said Jackie.

Theo said, "There's a piano out there if you get antsy." He laughed.

Mary Pat said, "And I get to be with my husband!" She and Samuel were sharing a loveseat. "What are the chances?"

Samuel said, "Good enough, apparently."

Theo said, "There should be a rule against that."

"Agreed," said Samuel. Mary Pat gave him a light elbow.

Dr. Tilton jumped in. "As we all know, today is not about music. It's about getting to know one another better. To that end, this first session's activity is one we haven't tried before. Courtesy of Gretchen, who suggested it."

Samuel said, "What is it? Did I miss something?"

Mary Pat said, "*Somebody* wasn't paying attention."

Samuel said, "Then tell me what it is, why don't you?"

Mary Pat said, "We're supposed to admit something we've done in chorus that nobody knows about, and we're not proud of. Any chorus."

"Thanks, Gretchen," said Theo with a sarcastic fist pump.

"Sounds fun to me," said Samuel.

"Me too," said Janey. "Can't wait."

Eleanor said, "Who wants to go first?"

"I will," said Mary Pat. "But it'd be a lot easier if our director wasn't in the room."

Samuel said, "Then I'll go first. I have no problem with it."

Mary Pat said, "No, no, I'll go. But you all know what I mean." She looked around the circle as Janey, Eleanor, Theo, and Jackie nodded.

Dr. Tilton said, "Pretend I'm not here."

"That's easier said than done," said Eleanor.

Mary Pat said, "Here goes." She put her hands on her knees. "About fifteen years ago, I had a concert with our church choir, and the day before, I'd tested positive for strep throat, but I didn't tell anybody. I just took painkillers and antibiotics and showed up and sang."

Eleanor said, "You could've infected the whole group!"

"They needed me," said Mary Pat. "But I shouldn't have done it."

Samuel said, "You never told me about that."

Mary Pat said, "Yes I did, but you weren't paying attention."

Samuel shook his head. Dr. Tilton said, "It sounds like everyone survived, and what a way to kick things off! Who's next?"

Eleanor said, "Let's go around the circle. Samuel?"

"Sure," said Samuel. "Let me think." They waited while he held his head in his hands. "I've got it." He looked up. "I lost the music for one of our songs, and I went to the library box and took somebody else's. I scratched out their number and wrote my own."

Janey said, "If it was in the box, they didn't need it."

Samuel said, "It was only the second week of rehearsal. The person hadn't collected their music yet."

Eleanor said, "Whose was it?"

Samuel said, "I don't know."

Eleanor said, "Well, what number was it?"

"I'm not saying," said Samuel.

Mary Pat elbowed him again. "Come on, Samuel."

"You come on."

Dr. Tilton said, "It may have been no one's. Not all numbers are assigned."

Samuel said, "Maybe so. But still, I shouldn't have done it."

"I agree," said Eleanor.

Theo said, "Well done, Samuel!" and laughed. "Okay, ready? I don't know if...oh, what the heck. I think it was my second year...the spring cycle. One of the concerts was on the same day as a basketball game that I really wanted to watch. It was an NCAA tournament game."

Samuel said, "I remember that. Bad scheduling." Mary Pat made a face.

Theo said, "Yeah, so...I told everyone I couldn't make the concert because I had a funeral to attend. Which was a lie, obviously."

"A funeral," said Eleanor with disapproval.

Theo said, "The worst part was...well, there were two things. One, my team lost. And two, the next day, at the Sunday concert, everyone in the choir was saying, 'I'm sorry for your loss.' I felt like a real jerk."

Janey said, "Why didn't you just record the game? And watch it later?"

Theo said, "Yeah, I could have. But I didn't." He looked at Dr. Tilton. "That's the only concert I've ever missed, though."

Janey said, "At least you're a bass, and not a tenor."

Everyone nodded. Theo said, "That's what I told myself at the time. But it was a bad decision, and I'm not proud." He turned to Eleanor. "Your turn."

Eleanor said, "I can't think of anything."

Theo said, "Really? There must be *something*. You've been doing this for how long?"

Dr. Tilton said, "I'll go next. We can come back to Eleanor."

Eleanor said, "Thanks, Armand."

Dr. Tilton said, "It was many years ago, in my university choir."

Theo said, "This oughta be good."

Janey said, "Right?"

Dr. Tilton continued, "I'd prepared diligently for a solo audition, but told my fellow tenors that I hadn't prepared at all. So if I flubbed the audition, I'd have an excuse."

Mary Pat said, "And what happened?"

"I aced the audition and got the part."

"Of course you did," said Eleanor.

Janey said, "Do you think anyone suspected?"

Dr. Tilton said, "Most likely, yes, if only because they'd all done the same thing at some point. Still, I wasn't proud of it then, and I'm not proud of it now."

Theo said, "It must feel good to finally get it off your chest."

Dr. Tilton thought for a moment. "No. Not really." He smiled and turned to Jackie. "Next."

Jackie said, "Yeah, okay. This was at my last accompanist gig, with another choir here in town. You all know which one."

"Mm-hm," said Eleanor.

Jackie said, "I'd forgotten to bring a pencil to rehearsal, so I stole one from a soprano."

"That's no biggie," said Janey. "I've stolen pencils."

Theo said, "Right there with you, Janey."

Jackie said, "It gets worse. When the soprano realized her pencil was missing, she looked around and saw mine. She pointed at it and said, 'Is that my pencil?' And I said, 'No.' I lied to her face. And then I let her borrow the pencil—her pencil—to make marks when she needed to."

"Oof," said Janey.

Mary Pat said, "I'm surprised no one in the choir had a spare pencil."

Theo said, "She was probably too ashamed to ask. Being a soprano." He laughed.

Eleanor said, "What are you implying?"

"Nothing," said Theo. "Never mind."

Dr. Tilton said, "Singers, let's make sure we aren't mining humor at others' expense."

Theo held up both hands. "Sorry, won't happen again." He looked at Janey. "Your turn."

"Okay," said Janey. "My thing is, I've purposefully avoided learning the solfege scale in reverse. Even though we do it in warmups like half the time."

Mary Pat said, "But it's so easy. Just write it down, and within a few..."

Samuel interrupted, "Don't be patronizing, Mary."

Mary Pat raised her voice. "Don't tell me what to do."

An awkward silence fell over the room. Dr. Tilton said, "Janey...I didn't know you were so opposed to solfege."

Janey said, "I'm not, really...or I guess I am, I don't know. I know I *should* learn it. I just haven't, and I'm not proud."

"There's always tomorrow," said Dr. Tilton.

Janey said, "Anyway, we're still waiting to hear Eleanor's thing." She looked at Eleanor. "You're the only one who hasn't admitted to something."

Eleanor said, "*I'm* still waiting to find out the number of the music Samuel took."

Everybody looked at Samuel. He said, "Alright, then. It was lucky number thirteen."

"I *knew* it!" said Eleanor. "That's *my* number!"

Theo said, "What are the chances?" and laughed.

Eleanor said, "That was the year I missed the first two weeks with a strained rib muscle."

Samuel said, "Sorry, Eleanor. Don't take it personally."

Mary Pat said, "Yeah, Eleanor. I don't."

Jackie said, "I didn't know choirs *had* a number thirteen."

"I requested it," said Eleanor. "I don't go in for superstitious nonsense."

Janey said, "Quit stalling, Eleanor. We want to hear something you're not proud of."

Eleanor sat up straighter. "Well, I'm sorry to tell you. There isn't anything."

Janey said, "You're saying your behavior's been perfect? I call BS on that."

"Seconded," said Theo.

"Thirded," said Samuel.

Mary Pat said, "Stay out of it, Samuel."

"*You* stay out of it."

"Singers..." said Dr. Tilton.

"Maybe this wasn't such a good idea," said Theo.

Janey said, "Go ahead, Eleanor."

Eleanor said, "I told you..."

They heard a knock at the door. It opened, and Gretchen, a soprano, was there. "How'd it go?" she said.

"Depends who you ask," said Theo.

Janey said, "We never heard from Eleanor. Apparently, her record is spotless."

Eleanor looked at Gretchen. "It went fine. And your timing is perfect." ♪

The Audition

The altos quit jabbering when Dr. Tilton clapped his hands. "Choir, we have...a new singer joining us!" The forty or so in attendance sat up straighter. "A tenor!" he said.

Oohs and aahs floated up. Theo said, "Yee-haw!"

Dr. Tilton said, "His name is Fabrizio, and he's..." He pointed. "He's right here!"

Everyone turned. Fabrizio was standing in the doorway. He looked like an Italian fashion model. He waved and flashed a gorgeous smile.

The altos started up again. Dr. Tilton said, "Wait, wait, choir...please!" Fabrizio was still at the threshold. "Fabrizio Gunther," said Dr. Tilton. (He pronounced it "Goonter.") "Did I say that right?"

"You said it flawlessly," said Fabrizio, in a voice that was crisp and clear and devoid of any accent.

"Come in!" said Dr. Tilton. He gestured to the six men and Janey in the third quadrant—going from his left to his right—of singers. "Stand, tenors!"

The tenors stood up. Fabrizio went over and shook the hand of each. He got to Janey last. "You're a tenor?" he said.

"For the time being," she said.

"Awesome," he said with eye contact and a smile. Janey's decision to bolster the tenor section suddenly felt better than it had.

Dr. Tilton said, "Have a seat next to Will." He pointed to a chair that held a sweatshirt and keys.

"Sure, yeah," said Will. He set his things on the floor. Fabrizio sat down. Even in the chair he was tall. He opened his folder. Dr. Tilton said, "Fabrizio insisted on having the music prior to tonight's rehearsal, so he could hit the ground running."

Fabrizio said, "I like to hit the ground running," and laughed. Most of the choir laughed with him. Janey laughed too, although she wasn't sure why.

Dr. Tilton said, "Among his other talents, Fabrizio knows solfege like the back of his hand." There were scattered groans. This time the altos' jabbering spilled over to the sopranos, then the basses. Dr. Tilton clapped twice and said, "How about some singing, yes?"

They went through the warmups. Janey was behind and one seat over from Fabrizio, but she could hear him well enough. His voice was robust and smooth. Like his cheekbones. Then Dr. Tilton called for the Brahms, a choral standard that Fabrizio must have sung previously, because he was hitting all the pitches and dynamics. The altos nodded with approval, already disarmed by his preparation and confidence.

At the break, Fabrizio was surrounded by those choir members who liked talking to newcomers. Other singers kept their distance, understanding that there would be plenty of time to get to know Fabrizio should he decide to stay. And that was the question in most minds: Are *we* good enough for *him*?

The first piece after the break was a contemporary offering by Sarah Quartel. Dr. Tilton said, "Let's go to measure fifty-two. Remember, choir, when we're singing quarter-note triplets, we subdivide the half rest as so." He demonstrated. "Understood?" Fabrizio nodded with the group. "Let's try it," said Dr. Tilton.

Jackie gave the starting pitches on the piano. Dr. Tilton counted off. The choir sang the passage.

Somebody was off. A few people looked at Fabrizio. Janey did too. He was smiling.

"Once again," said Dr. Tilton. He counted. Again, one singer was out of sync. It was Fabrizio. The altos murmured.

Dr. Tilton said, "Let's move on. We'll come back to this next week." As if he didn't want to put Fabrizio on the spot in his first rehearsal. This approach made sense to Janey—it must be a misunderstanding that would get cleared up over the coming days.

Fabrizio returned to competency for the remainder of the evening. By the end, Janey, and probably the altos, too, had given him a pass on those quarter-note triplets.

Janey was opening her car door when she heard her name. She turned around. It was Fabrizio. "Yes?" she said.

She was aware of Hazel, a soprano, watching from across the parking lot.

Fabrizio smiled. "Hey, Janey, it's cool to sing with you."

All she could think to say was, "You too."

He said, "I know you're not the section leader, but I could hear you all evening, and I *love* the way you sing tenor." He smiled wider.

Janey felt herself blush. Good thing it was nighttime.

Fabrizio said, "I was thinking you could help me with the music."

Janey looked as if she didn't know what that meant.

He said, "Since I'm coming in late. I have some catching up to do."

She said, "I thought you sounded good...er... what I heard."

"Thanks," he said. "Anyway, could we maybe get together for coffee sometime this week?"

"Oh, okay..."

"To go over a few things," he said.

She remembered the quarter-note triplets. "Okay...yeah."

"Cool. I look forward to it." The smile again.

They exchanged numbers. Fabrizio opened Janey's car door and held it as she got in. He went off to wherever his car was parked, and she drove away. She noted in her rearview mirror that Hazel hadn't moved.

As she drove home to her apartment, she couldn't help but wonder: Did he just ask me out on a date?

No. Not a date. He needs help with quarter-note triplets.

So why not ask Elroy, the section leader? Or Dr. Tilton even?

There was chemistry between them, wasn't there?

How fun and interesting and exciting! She called Rochelle, a soprano and her best friend in the choir. Rochelle said, "I saw you talking to the sexy new guy."

Janey laughed. "I thought just Hazel was watching."

"We were all watching."

"Great."

Rochelle said, "So…was he just making small talk, or what?"

"He wants help with the music."

"Ooh. That sounds fishy in a good way."

They analyzed the situation fully, even deciding what Janey was going to wear when she met Fabrizio—it gave her a little tingle to say his name—for their "date."

♪ ♪ ♪

Fabrizio greeted Janey on the patio of the locally owned coffee shop. "Thank you for coming," he said. He didn't try to hug her. Another perfect handshake. "You look great," he said. She blushed. This time he had to have noticed.

They took their folders inside and waited at the counter. Fabrizio talked about his previous choral experience and his hometown, which he'd left a few months earlier. When they got to the front of the line, he offered to pay. Janey put up modest resistance before letting him.

They took their lattes to the patio. Janey opened her music to the Quartel. She showed it to Fabrizio. "This is the one, right?"

He looked at it. "What do you mean?"

"This was what...one of things you wanted help with? The triplets?" She pointed at measure fifty-two.

Fabrizio furrowed his brow. "What about them?"

Now Janey was confused. "Oh...I thought..." She trailed off.

"Those are no big deal," he said.

"Well...Dr. Tilton is very particular when it comes to..."

He interrupted. "You're saying I was doing them wrong?"

She hesitated. "I mean...yeah."

He smiled and said, "You must have heard somebody else."

She stared at him.

He said, "Where should we go, anyway?"

"What?"

"To do this," he said. "Do you have a piano at your place?"

"No. I assumed we'd just...you know, do it here." She looked around. There were other occupied tables, but they were across the patio.

He shrugged. "Okay, whatever."

Janey pointed again at measure fifty-two. "Could you…um…speak the text in rhythm? These four bars?"

"What for?"

"Just…making sure."

"If that's what you need…" He opened to the page.

She counted off. He did it wrong. She said, "I see the problem. You're going dotted eighth, dotted eighth, eighth. And these are quarter-note triplets."

"I know what they are," he said.

"So…"

"They're not that different," he said.

Janey shifted in her seat. "Actually, they're completely different."

"You sound like a music director." He laughed.

She frowned. "I thought you wanted help."

"Yeah. And I thought you'd be cool. Not nitpicky."

Janey's heart rate increased. "Nitpicky? Are you for real right now?"

He smiled and put up a hand. "Easy, Janey. It's not like you're my section leader."

Janey closed her folder and stood up quickly, bumping the table and knocking over her latte. It spilled out from under the lid, through the wire tabletop, and onto the brick. She said, "You're an asshole, you know that?" She turned and left.

He called out, "Don't worry, I'll clean it up!"

The other patrons looked over. Janey got in her car, backed out of the parking space, and sped off.

She called Rochelle and recounted it all, ending with "What should I do?"

"That's a tough one," said Rochelle. "Did you really call him an asshole?"

Janey sighed. "Yeah."

She thought about calling Dr. Tilton, but for what? To tell him she'd had a bad date with the brand-new tenor? Her stomach turned. Should she text Fabrizio an apology? What if he decided not to join because of her?

She didn't know what to do, so she did nothing.

♪ ♪ ♪

Janey walked into the following week's rehearsal at six-thirty on the dot. Fabrizio's chair was empty. The altos were jabbering and looking over. Were they looking at her?

Dr. Tilton gave a loud clap. "Choir, choir. I have two announcements. One, please remember to send in your virtual recordings by the end of next week. Most of you have already done so, and I'm happy to say the project is coming along even better than I'd hoped. It will be a splendid addition to our website. And, secondly, I'm sorry to say...Fabrizio will *not* be joining us this cycle."

Someone said, "Why not?"

Dr. Tilton pretended not to hear. "Time for warmups," he said.

At the break, Janey went straight to Dr. Tilton, preempting the swarm. She said, "What happened with Fabrizio?"

Dr. Tilton said, "It wasn't a good fit."

"Did you decide that? Or did he?" Janey caught herself. "If you don't mind me asking."

Dr. Tilton lowered his voice. "I heard some things I didn't like at last week's rehearsal, so I called him back in for another audition. Turns out I'd been a little hasty."

Janey said, "Oh...what day was that?"

Dr. Tilton tilted his head. "Why do you ask?"

"Er, no reason. I was just...never mind."

Janey left Dr. Tilton and went outside. Rochelle saw her and came over. "What happened with Fabrizio? Did you find out?"

"He didn't make the cut," said Janey.

"Hah. So you were right, basically."

"I guess," said Janey.

"What're you gonna say if he calls you?"

Janey looked through the open door at Dr. Tilton holding court.

"I'm pretty sure he won't." ♪

Too Many Takes

Marnie put the phone on the tripod claw thingy and engaged the lock. She hit the button to use the front-side camera. The distance and framing were right, but the lighting was harsh.

She turned off the overhead cans and turned on two lamps. She sat in front of the phone. Now it was too dark. A different room, maybe? No, the dining room was the only place with a decent background. Anywhere else in the house, she'd have to move furniture.

She retrieved a third lamp from the bedroom and set it behind the tripod. She checked the image. Not perfect, but good enough for this virtual choir recording. It'd have to be.

She saw on the phone screen that her hair was doing something funny. She went into the bathroom to fix it. She stared at herself in the mirror. Hopefully the camera would capture what she was seeing right here.

She went back and opened her laptop. She clicked on the link. Sheet music took up most of the screen, with Dr. Tilton conducting at the top. Pretty neat, actually. This might even be fun. She took a sip from her water bottle, put in her earbuds, and pressed record on the phone. She tapped the space bar on the laptop.

She felt disconnected from the start but plowed through to the end. It didn't matter how good this first pass was. She just needed a basic idea of what it felt like, and how she looked and sounded.

She listened to the playback. She'd been prepared to dislike what she heard, but this was...awful. Not only was her voice raw and thin, but her tuning was off. Was this how she really sounded? On top of how she looked, with those embarrassing faces.

She reminded herself that her perception was skewed—she couldn't evaluate herself with objectivity. She also reminded herself that Dr. Tilton wouldn't let her sing in his group if she wasn't competent. There were plenty of other sopranos in town who'd love to have her chair, and she ought to feel grateful, not sorry for herself.

She would do the best she could. As for the weird faces, well...she'd have to let that part go.

She shook out her arms and did a few lip trills. She set aside her doubts.

Her voice cracked at the first entrance. Dammit! Okay. Now *that* was out of the way. She reset the devices and started again.

This time she was cruising. Feeling the music. During the easy middle section of the piece, she thought ahead to a harder passage that sometimes gave her trouble. The moment of distraction led her to sing "heat" instead of "heart." Double dammit! And it had been going so well! She stopped the recording.

She'd sung this piece through lots of times. She could do it on camera, couldn't she? Of course she could. Besides, Dr. Tilton had promised that no one would stick out. He'd said there were editing tools to "fix" things that needed fixing. She was comforted by the concept.

She gave herself a break by doing household chores. An hour later, she was ready to try again.

After several false starts, she was halfway into a take that was going well until she heard the squawk of a woodpecker. She hit stop. What the hell? She couldn't get a break! How was she supposed to make a decent recording if she needed the silent cooperation of a bird? Not to mention a motorcycle or an airplane?

She went to the living room and lay down on the couch. She was making this way too complicated. It was just a virtual choir recording. Choirs like hers made them all the time. Her only obstacle was herself.

She closed her eyes. She let herself drift off.

She woke up twenty minutes later, refreshed and determined. She checked her hair in a hallway mirror and marched back to the dining room. It was time to do this right. Right damn now.

She made it through a whole take without any major flubs. It was good enough, for sure. She didn't even allow herself to listen, knowing that if she did, she'd hate how she sounded. She resolved to submit the take before she changed her mind. If it wasn't acceptable, Dr. Tilton would let her know. It was his decision, not hers.

She was about to send the mpeg to the shared drive when she noticed something on the opening still frame. Huh? What is *that*? She zoomed in.

She put her fingers up to her face and felt dried drool on her cheek. Oh, Christ!

Calm down, she told herself. It was fine, nobody would notice. She'd be one of thirty or forty people on a screen. Her image would be small.

But wouldn't Dr. Tilton feature different singers in close-ups? Of course he would. Like every other virtual choir she'd seen. Then again, she could add a note requesting that she not be featured at any point. He'd respect that, wouldn't he? There were plenty of other singers to showcase.

No, no, no! She wasn't going to send out a video of herself with spit on her face. Under any circumstances. She went into the bathroom and scrubbed the chalky whiteness from her cheek with a hand towel. She touched up her makeup and went back for one last try. If this didn't work, she'd...Don't think about that! Focus on the task. She pressed play.

She botched the first chorus. She reset and started again.

She botched the first verse. She couldn't get out of her head. It was just music, for crying out loud! She closed the laptop in frustration and went outside to get the mail.

A drink might do the trick. Just a little one, to take the edge off. She opened a bottle of wine and poured a half-serving. She took a sip, and her stress melted away. She could do this! She absolutely could. Besides, she wasn't ready to accept the alternative—having to live with herself if she gave up.

She put the glass in the sink and went back to her station for what she hoped was the last time. It had better be.

Her first entrance was flawless, the best she'd ever sung it. She went on, buoyed with confidence. She was doing her part and doing it well.

The last page—almost there! She heard a noise. What?

The creak of the back door. She stopped singing.

Keys dropped on a table.

She put her head in her hands. Robbie was home, and the perfect take was ruined.

Robbie poked his head in and saw the setup. "Oh, sorry," he said. "I hope I didn't screw up your recording."

She looked at him. "You did, actually."

"How was I supposed to know?"

Her voice was edgy. "You knew I was doing this today."

"It's two-thirty," he said. "You said you were doing it in the morning. I didn't think..." He shook his head.

She looked at the time on her phone. "Shit, I've been doing this all freaking day! Literally, and I have nothing to show for it."

He came over and put a hand on her shoulder. "I'm sorry. I can go to the bedroom. Or back out if you want."

"No, I'm done for now. I'll try again another time." She closed the laptop.

"I'm really sorry," he said.

"It's not your fault." She put her hand on his.

After dinner she called fellow soprano Susannah to tell her about the fiasco.

"It can't be that bad," said Susannah. "You're a great singer."

"Trust me, it *is* that bad." Marnie took Susannah through her day of mishaps, many of which Susannah could relate to. By the end, they were both laughing. Marnie said, "Did you do yours? How did it go?"

Susannah said, "It went fine. I ended up using my third take."

"That doesn't make me feel any better."

"I've done these before. Isn't this your first time?"

"Yeah," said Marnie. Even her speaking voice sounded worn.

Susannah said, "How about you send me one of your takes? I'm sure it's way better than you think."

"It's not, I promise."

"Just send it."

Marnie thought about what she'd saved. "I guess I could send you my first run-through. It's the only take where I made it to the end. Besides the one with the drool."

"Okay, send it."

"No," said Marnie. "It's not close to good enough."

"I want to hear it anyway."

"Why?"

"Because I do," said Susannah.

"Will you be honest about it? Because if you're not..."

"Totally honest," said Susannah. "I promise."

"Should I be careful what I wish for?"

"Come on, Marnie. Just send it."

"I'll think about it."

"Don't think," said Susannah. "Send."

Marnie took a long time to respond. "Fine, I will."

"While I'm on the phone."

Marnie said, "Hold on one sec." Susannah waited. "There, it went."

"Great," said Susannah. "I'm going out now, but I'll be able to listen first thing in the morning. Can you wait for that?"

"Sure. Not like it matters, anyway."

"Okay, I'll call you tomorrow. Keep your head up."

♪ ♪ ♪

Later that night, Marnie opened her inbox to an email.

Marnie,

Thank you for your recording. It was among the best I received. The choir and I are lucky to have you. Keep up the good work.

With song and light, Armand

♪

I Know That Brand

Will never had throat lozenges, because he rarely needed them. And when he did, there were plenty of other choir members who were fully stocked and willing to share. But his throat was bothering him *now*.

His wife would have some. She was more of a lozenge person than he was, even though she'd never sung in any capacity. Not that she couldn't—she just didn't.

He went to the pantry. He pulled out a large plastic bin and took off the top. It was stuffed to the point of annoyance, as usual. Cassandra was a hoarder when it came to pharmaceuticals. Acetaminophen, ibuprofen, cough syrups, cold remedies, Band-Aids, creams, etc., etc. But no lozenges. How?

He jogged to the master bath with a flicker of hope. He opened the small cabinet above his wife's side of their matching sinks, and...there. A small cylindrical package, honey-flavored. Perfect. He unscrewed the cap and dumped one out. It was pale yellow. He put it in his mouth. It tasted a little funny but would do the trick. He stuck the tube in his pocket in case he needed more later and drove to rehearsal.

The lights and traffic cooperated, and he pulled into the parking lot a few minutes early. Singers were locking their cars and trudging toward the church's side building. Parked to his left and rummaging through her glove compartment was Hazel. She lowered her window closest to him, and he lowered his. She said, "I can't believe I forgot my lozenges. Eleanor says she can't spare any, but I'm suspicious. Who doesn't have extra lozenges?"

"I have extra lozenges," he said. There was pride in his voice.

"Really?" said Hazel. "What kind are they?"

"These." He stuck out his arm and showed her the packet. "They're honey-flavored." Hazel squinted at it in the fading light. Will got out and waited as she reorganized and closed the glove compartment. They met at his bumper.

"I know that brand," she said.

"My wife knows her lozenges."

"I guess so," said Hazel. She put her folder in her armpit and stuck out a hand.

Will tipped a lozenge into her palm. She studied it. He said, "I'm just finishing one up right now." He pushed out his cheek with his tongue. "And I'm still alive." He smiled.

"Thank you," she said. She placed the thing in her mouth. She sucked on it for a few seconds and made a face. "It has an odd taste."

"It's not candy," he said.

"No, it's not," she said, and headed in. He walked alongside her, silent but pleased.

He sat down in the tenor section and turned to Janey. "Lozenge?" he said, showing her the container.

She glanced at it. "No, thanks. I don't take lozenges from strange men."

Will couldn't come up with a snappy comeback, so he turned to Elroy and Daniel behind him. "How about you guys?"

Elroy said, "Don't mind if I do." Will shook one into Elroy's palm.

"I'll take one, too," said Daniel.

Will then offered up the tube to the altos, but they smiled and shook their heads. Two of them produced packets of their own.

About ten minutes into rehearsal, Will noticed Dr. Tilton's hair. It was longer than usual and doing a wispy thing behind the ears that made him look like a terrier.

Dr. Tilton the terrier. Funny. Not just funny, hilarious. While the terrier was instructing the altos on a vowel sound, Will leaned toward Janey and said, "Check out Tilton's hair." Janey shook her head, stone-faced. Will snickered and turned to Elroy, who was staring at his music.

Will looked over at the sopranos. He caught Hazel's eye and smiled. She smiled back. He decided that Hazel and he could actually be friends, in spite of the age difference, and the personality difference, and…maybe they weren't so different after all. He looked around the room. He realized that all these people of whom he'd formed various and shifting opinions were fundamentally good and were there to make music, like him, for the love of it. He realized there was no place he'd rather be in that moment than right where he was.

Dr. Tilton faced the front. "Let's try it again," he said. "Tutti." He counted off.

The ensemble sang through a section they'd been struggling with for weeks, and suddenly it sounded perfect. Will was watching the wisps of hair and started to giggle. He stopped singing, completely overtaken by laughter. Dr. Tilton cut off the group and made a this-had-better-be-good face. "What's so funny, Will?"

Will's elation turned into self-consciousness. Everyone was looking. He'd interrupted rehearsal. And he couldn't explain it out loud—Dr. Tilton the terrier? He sought comfort by looking at his new friend Hazel. She was red-faced and sweaty, and her eyes showed alarm. She closed her folder and used it to fan herself. Rochelle, seated next to her, said, "Hazel, are you okay?"

Hazel said, "Why is it so darn warm in here?"

Dr. Tilton said, "What is going on this evening?"

Hazel leaned forward, and her folder slid to the floor. The altos made worried noises. Rochelle put a hand on Hazel's shoulder and shook gently. "Hazel?"

Hazel sat up and waved her hands. "I'm alright, I'm alright. I just got nauseous. A little bit."

I KNOW THAT BRAND

Rochelle said, "Could it be something you ate?"

Hazel said, "I haven't had anything since lunch."

Eleanor said, "Maybe your blood pressure dropped due to lack of sugar."

Georgia, the altos' section leader and an actual physician, went over and knelt beside Hazel. "Is it possible you're dehydrated?"

Hazel said, "No, I don't think so." She pointed to the water bottle by her feet, which was half-full.

Georgia said, "Are you taking any medications?"

"Not at the moment. I mean…I had a lozenge."

"What kind of lozenge?" said Georgia.

Will started digging into his pocket.

Elroy yelled out, "Eureka!" Everyone looked at him. He said, "I know what it feels like to be stoned, and I can tell you, right now…"

Will held up the packet. "It was one of these," he said. "I had one too." His voice was whiny. "This is a good brand."

"I know that brand," said Eleanor.

"So do I," said Georgia.

Elroy took the tube from Will and removed the top. He stuck his nose in and sniffed. "I knew something was off. It's just been a long time since I…you know."

Janey took the tube and smelled it also. "Yup," she said. "We have a diagnosis."

Will said, "Are you saying they're *pot* lozenges?"

Elroy nodded. "That's exactly what they are."

"Oh, my," said Daniel, another physician and the board president.

Theo said, "Just when I thought I'd seen it all," and laughed.

The altos started jabbering. Dr. Tilton clapped twice and said, "Choir...how many of you took those lozenges?" Will, Elroy, Daniel, and Hazel raised their hands. Dr. Tilton said, "Alright, let's take a break, and I'll figure out what to do."

Most of the choir got up. Several singers gathered around Hazel, who seemed to be feeling much better. Janey handed the container back to Will. "Looks like you messed up."

Will nodded, frowning. His perfect moment was gone. He could feel the thoughts of the entire chorus, judging. He stood up and spoke. "I'm really, really sorry. I had no idea." He stared at the lozenges, as if doing so would somehow excuse what had happened, and put them in his pocket. He went straight out the door, forgetting his music.

What a mess.

His wife was already in bed, but still awake. He dropped the tube on the pillow next to her. He'd thought about what to say the entire drive home. "I accidentally gave away three of your pot lozenges at rehearsal. You can imagine how that went." Cassandra sat up, looking like she'd swallowed an egg. He said, "I don't see how I can ever show my face there again." Cassandra didn't say anything. He said, "Why didn't you tell me?" He raised his voice. "And why in the world would you hide them in an effing regular container?"

"I thought you'd judge me," she said.

Will picked up the lozenges and threw them back down on the bed. "You're effing right I'm effing judging you! How about some common sense? Jesus!" He stormed off to the kitchen. Aside from everything else, he was ravenous.

He made himself a quick sandwich. As he ate, it occurred to him that maybe he shouldn't have gone into her cabinet to begin with. He brushed off his hands, took a deep breath, and went back to her. She hadn't moved. He sat on the bed. "Please tell me why," he said.

"I haven't been sleeping well, so I got a...I got some to try. I was embarrassed to tell you."

"But...you know I have nothing against weed. I just don't do it because of my job."

"Will this get you in trouble at school?" she said.

"No, no. Don't worry about that. It's just...people in the choir know I'm a teacher. It's mortifying."

She stared down at her hands.

"You should've told me," he said. "We're married, aren't we?"

She nodded without looking up.

He put a hand on her arm. "Is there...something more we need to talk about?"

She shook her head. "No...is everybody okay?"

"They're fine. It's only five milligrams, I think. But it totally blew up rehearsal."

She looked up. "Did it really? Oh, no."

"Yeah." He picked up the tube. "*I* was having a *great* time, actually, until..." He opened it. "Do you mind?"

"Seriously?" she said.

"Yeah," he said. "At this point, why not?"

"Go ahead, they're all yours."

He said, "No, they're yours. I'll replace the ones I took. Meanwhile, I need to come up with a story for how I got them."

"Tell them the truth. About your idiot wife."

"No, no," he said, tapping his chest. "I need to take responsibility. If I try and put it off on you...yeah, no. I'll come up with something." He was trying to remember exactly what he'd said to Hazel. Hopefully *she* wouldn't remember.

Cassandra said, "So...you're not gonna get, like, kicked out for this?"

"I don't see why. It was an accident. Plus, I'm a tenor." He smiled and held up the container. "You sure you don't want one of these?" He slid closer to her. "I promise I won't judge." ♪

The Solfege Olympiad[1]

David was lying in the dark, staring at the ceiling. Hal had rolled over, facing away. Like he did every night as soon as he got into bed.
    David said, "You still awake?"
    Hal said, "Trying not to be."
    "Can I rub your back?"
    "That *will* keep me awake," said Hal.
    "Okay. Let me know if you change your mind."
    Hal didn't respond.
    David said, "I think we should go to that thing in Akron. What Armand was talking about. The solfege olympics."
    Still no response. David repeated himself, louder.
    Hal said, "What part of 'I'm trying to sleep' do you not understand?"
    "We'd need to get flights now. It's this coming Saturday."
    "Are you seriously still talking?" said Hal.
    "We *need* to talk about it if we're gonna go. If we're even thinking about it."

---

1   The Solfege Olympiad takes place every four years.

"Christ, David. You're so selfish."

"I'm gonna look into plane tickets," said David. "Maybe we can use points." He turned on his phone. The screen was bright.

Hal rolled onto his back. "What...the hell...?"

"Didn't you hear Armand? He said...no, of course you didn't, because you were playing on your phone during announcements."

"I wasn't playing," said Hal. "I was organizing my calendar."

David sat up. "Why can't you ever just be a normal, present person during rehearsal? You're always distracted, and you don't know the music."

Hal said, "I get my act together come concert time. *Every* time. You should worry less about me and more about your own mediocre singing."

"Well, that's a shitty thing to say."

"Just telling it the way it is," said Hal.

"Do you have to be such a jerk?" said David.

Hal raised his voice. "A jerk? Really? Have I not sung in this stupid amateur choir for years, just for you? I don't even like it. In fact, I hate it."

"If it's beneath you and you hate it, then quit already. Instead of torturing me."

"Torturing? That is really...!" Hal threw off the covers and stood up. He grabbed his pillow. "I'm moving to the other room. Screw you and good night."

David said, "What about Akron?" but Hal was already out the door.

Seconds later, Hal poked his head in. "I wouldn't sit through a solfege competition if you paid me." He was gone again.

David yelled out, "Screw you, too!" and started looking for flights.

♪ ♪ ♪

Three days later, David was sitting at the lobby bar of the Hiatus Hotel and Suites in Akron. It was early evening. Most of the tables and at least half the barstools were occupied.

A woman came up next to him. She wore a purple T-shirt with the words *Repertory Singers of Dayton* on the front. She ordered a round of drinks from one of the bartenders.

David said, "I guess you're here for the solfege."

She smiled and patted her chest. "Yes, sir. I'm here with some peeps from my choir. They're over there." She pointed toward a dozen or so people in the same shirt as hers. "How about you? Are you competing?"

David shook his head. "No. I'm just here to watch."

"Oh. You're a singer, though, I bet."

"Yeah. I sing bass in an audition choir in Southern California."

"Wow, you've come a long way," she said. "You must really like solfege."

"I wouldn't say that. Just interested."

"Is anyone else here from your choir?" she said.

"Nope. Only me."

The bartender was ready with the drinks. The woman said, "Can you take them to our table please? Purple shirts."

"Sure can," he said.

She turned back to David. "I'm Edie, by the way. Feel free to join us if you get lonely."

"Thank you, I might. I'm David."

"Welcome to Ohio, David."

"Glad to be here," he said. "So you're competing, then?"

"Yes, sir. In the amateur ensemble division. We're on tomorrow at ten-thirty. And we're super excited."

"Well, I hope you win," said David.

"Thanks, but we won't. It'll be a blast, though." Something caught her eye, and she put a hand to her mouth. "There's Tido Lang! He's the two-time defending champion! Gotta go tell my peeps." She rushed back to her table.

David was thinking about another drink when a man sat on the stool next to him and stuck out a hand. "Oscar Lang," he said. "But everyone calls me Tido."

David accepted the handshake. "My name's David, and I'm only a spectator."

"That's great, man. We don't get many of those. Mostly pros like me and amateurs like them." He pointed a thumb at the Dayton table.

David said, "I understand you're the champ."

"That's right. And I still will be come Sunday morning."

"It's good to be confident."

"Yeah," said Tido. "Especially when it comes to solfege. If you show weakness, the competition will kill you and eat you."

David nodded. The whole thing was surreal.

Tido said, "Buy you a drink?"

David looked at his phone. No return call from Hal. He looked at Tido, who was well-built and handsome and had a sonorous bass voice. "Sure," he said. "Why not?"

They sat drinking and talking for hours, interrupted every so often by solfege enthusiasts looking for an autograph. It was clear Tido liked the attention. Meanwhile, David was glad he'd come. He and Hal had needed a break from each other. And a world-class singer was asking him if he wanted to come up to his room.

"I shouldn't," said David. He held up his left hand, thumbing his wedding band.

Tido smiled. "Come on, now. What happens in Akron stays in Akron."

David was considering it.

Tido said, "From what you've told me, you two are on the outs anyway. Might as well take advantage of your opportunities." He put a hand on David's knee.

David thought a little more. He was definitely drunk. "Alright...but only if I get a demonstration. I want to hear what all the fuss is about."

"How have you never heard me? I'm everywhere online."

David laughed. "I want a private demo. That's my condition."

Tido slid his hand up David's thigh. "Deal," he said.

♪ ♪ ♪

Tido was in the bathroom, "freshening up." David sat on the bed. He thought of Hal—gloomy and arrogant and not returning his calls—as he unbuttoned his shirt. He stripped down to his socks and boxers. He put his belt in one shoe and his phone, now off, in the other. He stacked his clothes atop his shoes and looked around.

There was room on the desk. He went over. Peeking out from the top of a folder was a page of sheet music. All he could see was the title, "Confirmation." He thought of his younger days in the church.

He heard the bathroom door open. He turned to see Tido, who was naked.

"What are you doing?" said Tido.

"Putting my clothes down."

Tido went over and tucked the sheet music back inside the folder. "You weren't going through my stuff, were you?"

"Of course not," said David. "Why would I do that?"

"Like I said, the competition is murder." Tido laughed. "Can't be too careful." He looked David up and down. "I guess the demonstration will have to wait." He put his hands on David's face and pulled him in.

♪ ♪ ♪

Light was peeking around the edges of the curtains when David woke up in his own room with a dry mouth and a headache. He checked his phone. He still hadn't heard from Hal. He felt a pit in his stomach. What had he done? He got out of bed, took eight hundred milligrams of ibuprofen, and got ready for what promised to be an interesting day.

He checked out and left his roller bag with the bellman. He spent the morning in the Sauerkraut Ballroom watching amateur ensembles. The same room hosted the amateur solo division after a lunch break. David was amazed at the skill of the contestants, both in groups and as soloists. Even the first-timers from Dayton had been impressive. If nothing else, his appreciation of what could be done with solfege had grown by an order of magnitude. He looked forward to telling Armand all about it.

He'd want to tell Hal, too, except Hal would probably make fun of it, and belittle him in the process. David considered that their marriage might be coming to an end. He wasn't even sad about it. More like numb.

A few minutes before four o'clock, the Goodyear Ballroom was packed and sizzling with energy. David hadn't gotten the demonstration he'd been promised, but it didn't matter now. Tido's division was up next. David went toward an empty seat near the back and almost bumped into Edie.

"Oh, hi!" she said.

"Remember me?" he said.

"Yes, sir. You made fast friends with Tido."

"He's a friendly guy."

"I got his autograph eight years ago," she said. "Before he'd even won the first time. I think that makes it extra meaningful."

David agreed and changed the subject. "You were great this morning. Really."

"Thank you. We try."

David looked at his phone. "Do you know how late this will go?"

"Not very. There's only sixteen pro qualifiers, same as the amateurs. Otherwise it would take too long."

"That makes sense," said David. He did some math in his head and decided he'd be able to stay for all of it.

Edie said, "You want to sit with us? We've got seats near the front, and I just found out one of us had to leave early."

David looked at the chairs filling up. "I'd like that, thank you."

♪ ♪ ♪

The professional solo division for the Eighth Solfege Olympiad had come down to four semifinalists: Sonja "Nightingale" Desmond, Peter "Piper" Wells, "Loony" Laura Holdsclaw, and Tido Lang.

Edie said, "I think it's gonna be Loony Laura. She's amazing, isn't she? But you can't count Tido out, either."

David nodded. He'd finally gotten to hear what Tido could do, and it was indeed impressive.

Edie said, "Piper Wells has no chance. He doesn't have the range, even though he's a tenor. And Nightingale must be having an off day. I've heard her sound much better."

"She still made the semis, though," said David.

"Of course she did. She's an ex-champ." Edie shouted, "Go Laura!"

Numbers were drawn from a basket, and each semifinalist was assigned an art song. All four songs were by the same composer, in this case Henry Purcell. The competitors had two minutes to look over the music, after which they had to sing a designated passage in solfege *a cappella*. Because this was *movable do*[2] solfege—as opposed to *fixed do*[3] solfege—the singers were not given a starting note. They could begin on the *do* of their choosing.

David couldn't distinguish between the performances quality-wise. The degree of solfege mastery on display was so far outside of his experience that it all sounded equally impossible. The judges, however, appeared confident in their scoring, and promoted Loony Laura and Tido to the finals.

"Here we go," said Edie. "For all the marbles." She raised a fist and shouted. "You can do it, Laura!" Loony Laura waved in their direction. Edie said, "Did you know she's from Canada? That's why she's called 'Loony.'"

---

2   where the tonic of the scale is *do*, regardless of key signature
3   where *do* is fixed at a certain note, regardless of key signature

"No, I didn't," said David. "Makes sense."

Minutes later, the composer for the final round was revealed as Charlie Parker.

"Charlie Parker," said Edie. "That's different."

"The saxophonist?" said David. All he knew of Charlie Parker was that he was a jazz legend and had died young. And there were drugs.

"Yeah," said Edie. "He must've written some pretty hard songs."

While Edie chatted with members of her group, David checked his phone. Still nothing from Hal. He googled Charlie Parker and started reading.

The chime sounded. It was time. Tido won the coin toss and opted to go second.

Loony Laura's passage was from a song called "Ornithology." Her performance sounded perfect to David, but the judges gave her a score of only 7.5 out of 10. "Does that seem low to you?" he asked Edie.

"The judges are all ex-champs or runners-up, so they know what they're doing."

It was Tido's turn. He had to sing a passage from "Donna Lee."

"I've heard *of* that, I think," said Edie. "But I don't think I've ever heard it."

"Me either," said David.

Tido brought down the house and earned a score of 9.5. It was the highest score in the history of the competition, and he'd won three straight titles.

Edie stood up. "Too bad. Oh, well. Are you staying for the afterparty?"

"No, I've got a plane to catch."

"Well, it was nice to meet you, David." She went over to talk to Loony Laura.

David looked at his phone. The Charlie Parker page was still showing. He scrolled down and saw a list of compositions. He stared at the word "Confirmation."

He remembered the music he'd seen the night before.

He remembered that Tido had acted strangely when he'd come out of the bathroom, and now David knew why: Tido had cheated. Somehow, he'd found out who the final composer was and had come prepared.

David looked at Tido, surrounded by fans. Should he tell someone? A judge? An organizer? But tell them what, exactly? That he'd seen an incriminating piece of sheet music during a one-night stand? It didn't prove anything on its own. And it could mess things up even more with Hal.

He went to the bellman and got his bag. He didn't want to see Tido. They hadn't traded contact info, and that's how it should remain. He pulled up his ride app and went outside.

♪ ♪ ♪

At the gate, David turned on his phone. There was a missed call from Hal. He dialed.

Hal answered. "I'm so glad you called," he said.

"You ghosted me." There was anger in David's voice.

"I know, and I'm sorry. I needed a break. I hope you understand."

"That was really shitty."

"You're right, it was," said Hal. "But I'll make it up to you. If you let me."

David softened. "I guess I needed a break, too."

"So get this. I worked on our choir music while you were gone. Wait 'til you hear me sing it."

David was silent.

"David? Honey?"

Hal hadn't called him that in years. David said, "Why did you do that? Work on the music?"

Hal said, "I know how important it is to you, and I want you to know that from now on, I'm going to take it just as seriously as you."

David said, "If you don't care about it, you don't care about it. You can't help that."

"I care about *you*," said Hal. "I love you, and I miss you, and I really hope we can work out our differences. I think we can."

David thought about the cheating that had gone on over the past twenty-four hours and decided: What had happened in Akron should stay in Akron.

"I love you, too," he said. ♪

Not Forgotten

The altos whispered to one another when the woman appeared, forty-five minutes before the end of rehearsal. It happened every once in a while, someone down on their luck wandering in and taking a seat by the door. As long as the person stayed quiet, Dr. Tilton didn't mind. But this woman was making noise, mumbling and tapping her feet to an unheard rhythm.

Some of the singers looked at the woman with concern while others looked away. Dr. Tilton said, "Excuse me, madam, you're welcome to stay and listen, but you'll need to be quiet."

The woman raised a hand and nodded. The mumbling stopped and the foot tapping became a silent twitch.

"Thank you," said Dr. Tilton. "Again, choir..."

Rehearsal continued, but Marnie was distracted. The woman was wrapped in layers of what looked like found clothing, including a wool hat and sunglasses with fake gems on the rims. Marnie wondered what her story was, and if everyone else in the choir was wondering the same thing.

"Sopranos," said Dr. Tilton. "From measure thirty-two."

They sang the passage. Marnie saw several basses—those nearest the woman—look over in surprise.

Dr. Tilton said, "Not bad sopranos, but you can do better. Again."

This time the woman sang loud enough for all to hear. Dr. Tilton said, "I'm sorry, madam, but this is your last warning. You must be completely silent." He paused. "Will that be possible?"

The woman raised her hand and nodded, like before. Her leg went still.

"Thank you," said Dr. Tilton. "Once more, sopranos." Marnie didn't sing, preferring instead to watch the woman mouth the words of a song that wasn't popular even by choral music standards.

After a few minutes, the woman got up and left. Marnie wondered where she was going. A community shelter? A breezeway, a park bench, a spot in the bushes? Why hadn't she stayed to the end, at least? Where it was safe, warm, and comfortable.

Marnie rushed out as soon as rehearsal was over. She poked around the sides and rear of the church, hoping to find the woman. Why so much interest? There was something about her. The way she raised her hand. Like some choral singers did when they made a mistake. And the way she mouthed those words.

Marnie thought of the hat and glasses. As if the woman didn't want to be recognized. Or seen, even.

Speaking of, Marnie would probably never see her again. She tried to forget about the whole thing and enjoy what remained of the evening.

The woman showed up the following week at the same time. She had on the same clothes as before, hat and glasses included. This second appearance drew a range of reactions from the singers, from acting like she wasn't there to empathetic whispers.

At 8:50, the woman left. Marnie got up and followed, avoiding eye contact with Dr. Tilton and Eleanor. A reason for the early exit could be concocted later. She made it outside just in time to see the woman disappear around the corner of the building. Marnie hurried to catch up. As she got close, the woman heard her and turned around.

"I was quiet, wasn't I?"

"Yes, you were," said Marnie. She stopped short, so as not to cause alarm. "I just wanted to say hello."

"What for?" said the woman.

"You came to listen twice," said Marnie. "It must mean something to you."

"I like music."

"I saw you mouthing the words. Are you a singer?"

"I used to be."

The woman took off her glasses. Even in the dark, her face showed signs of exposure. "What do you want?" she said. There was an edge to her voice.

"I want to help you," said Marnie.

"I don't need your help." The woman turned to leave.

"Wait," said Marnie. "Can I give you a ride somewhere? It's bad weather to be walking around."

"I'm used to it."

"Alright. Anyway, my name's Marnie."

"I don't need any more friends. Leave me alone."

"Okay. I just hope you have...somewhere to go."

"You can forget about me. Like everyone else."

Marnie hesitated, then held out her folder. "Would you like this?"

The woman stared at it. "You're giving me your music?"

"Yes, take it. I can get more copies."

"Fine," said the woman. She stepped forward and took the folder. "What should I do with it?"

Marnie said, "I don't know...look at it, I guess. And hear the music in your head."

The woman patted one side of the folder. "This could be good for sitting on."

Marnie said, "Oh...that's not..." She didn't know how to finish the sentence.

The woman said, "I don't want your help." Her face changed. "And don't follow me! I hate that!" She walked off and disappeared into the night.

On her way home, Marnie began to regret giving away her music. She could print new copies, yes, but her rehearsal notes were gone. She'd have to sit with another soprano to rewrite them. And why had she done it? So the woman could use the folder as a seat cushion on the ground? She'd acted without thinking.

The next morning, she got a call from Eleanor. During Marnie's year and a half in the choir, she'd never gotten a call from Eleanor, so it must be important. After they exchanged hellos, Eleanor said, "That homeless woman you chased after, her name is Patricia. She used to be a member of this choir. You're not the first person to try and help her."

"Oh…I had no idea."

"You can't believe anything she says," said Eleanor.

"Okay…" said Marnie. "Does Dr. Tilton know it was her?"

"Of course he does. Like most of us, he knew the moment she walked in. But what was he supposed to do? He treated her like he would anyone else coming in off the street."

"I guess…that makes sense."

Eleanor said, "Patricia and I were close. She came to my children's weddings. We traveled together. When her addiction took control, her whole life went down the toilet."

"Gosh," said Marnie. "Does she have any family?"

"She used to. She had everything, and now she has nothing. It's very, very sad."

After hanging up, Marnie felt foolish. She hadn't mentioned the folder out of embarrassment. She'd tried to be a hero, but her actions were misguided and unwanted. And now she'd have to spend hours recreating what she'd given away.

♪ ♪ ♪

A month passed without Patricia returning, but Marnie couldn't stop thinking about her. Each week, before and after rehearsal, she spent a few minutes looking. Why she did that, she didn't know. She had a vague idea she could help somehow, or the choir could. Or should.

The repertoire was getting close to concert ready when Patricia showed up the third Tuesday in November. She sat by the door, as usual, but this time she wasn't wearing the hat and glasses. Her hair was combed, and she carried a music folder.

Dr. Tilton clapped his hands. "Choir," he said. "Stand, please. We're going to run the Gjeilo."

The singers stood and opened their folders. Marnie watched Patricia do the same. Dr. Tilton cued Jackie, who played the intro. When the sopranos entered in bar nine, Patricia sang with them.

Dr. Tilton gave a cutoff. He said, "Patricia, I'm very sorry. We're preparing for a concert, and we don't have time or space for visiting singers."

Marnie spoke up. "I don't see the problem with her singing along. She obviously knows the piece."

Eleanor said, "The problem is, we're a section that's been singing together for the whole cycle. This isn't family choir at church."

Patricia raised her hand. "Never mind," she said. "I thought maybe you hadn't forgotten about me."

The altos and most everyone else looked at their shoes.

Dr. Tilton said, "I'm sorry, Patricia, but we can't help you. Not at the moment. If you stay after, I'm sure some of our members would love to speak with you. I guarantee you've been forgotten by no one."

Patricia set the folder on the chair and walked out. After a few seconds, Marnie handed her (new) music to Philip, a bass, and ran outside. She caught a glimpse of movement out by the curb. There! Marnie ran over. Patricia was walking away. Marnie said, "Patricia, please! We want to help you!"

Patricia spun around. "You heard Eleanor. They don't want me. And I don't want them!"

Marnie took a step toward Patricia, who shrieked. "Get away from me!" Marnie froze. Patricia said, "You're wrong about me! Got that? You're wrong!"

Marnie could do nothing but watch as Patricia went off down the street with a limp that hadn't been present before.

Marnie was near tears when she got back. The choir was singing, as rehearsal had continued. Marnie half-expected Dr. Tilton to give a cutoff when she entered, but he didn't. He went on as if nothing had happened. Marnie went to her seat, found her place in the music, and joined in. What else was there to do?

At the end of rehearsal, Theo went over and picked up the folder Patricia had left behind. He opened it. "It's empty," he said. He looked closer. "This belongs to... Marnie?" He looked up and saw Marnie, who was crying.

Susannah said, "What happened, Marn?"

Marnie didn't respond, but went over to Theo and took the folder. She kept going, out the door and to her car.

She thought of what Eleanor had said: *You can't believe anything she says.*

Sitting in her driveway, Marnie turned on the car's dome light and examined the folder. The outsides were badly scuffed and dirty, and the binder rings were bent. As if it had been sat on. ♪

ONCE IN A LULLABY

Armand pulled into the assisted living facility parking lot at four p.m. Visitors were permitted throughout the day, but his mother seemed at her best in the afternoon hours before dinner.

The front desk attendant was a woman Armand didn't recognize. "Hello there," he said, trying to sound cheerful. He wasn't cheerful, though. It was his third or fourth visit to the place, and he didn't like it. Not that there was anything wrong—the staff seemed competent and caring—but he wished he had the resources to get his mother in-home care instead.

The attendant pointed to a clipboard at the edge of the desk. "Sign in, please. Who are you here to see?"

"Dottie Tilton. I'm her son, Armand. I don't believe we've met." He stuck a hand across the counter.

The attendant waved. "We try to limit physical contact. It's part of our health and wellness policy."

Armand pulled his hand back. "Of course! I knew that. It's a reflex." He wrote his name and the time on the log-in sheet. "And your name is...?"

"Sorry, I'm Kathy." She sighed. "It's been a day."

"I'm sorry to hear that. It must be a challenging job you have."

"At times, yes." She half-smiled.

Armand followed her across the large main room, a living area with a television connected to an open kitchen and a pair of dining tables. Against one wall was an upright piano, which Armand had considered opening but hadn't yet. Three residents, two in wheelchairs and one in a recliner, were watching the local news, joined by several of someone's family members on a couch. Kathy went down a hallway and stopped at the second doorway on the left. The door was open.

"She's awake," said Kathy, gesturing for Armand to come ahead. "But she's had a rough day so far."

Armand wondered if his mother could hear what Kathy was saying. Probably not, at her age, but he'd noticed only minimal signs of hearing loss and would rather err on the side of caution. He beckoned Kathy away from the door.

He said, "Anything special?"

"No, nothing special. Argumentative, wouldn't eat any lunch."

"Oh," he said. "I'm sorry on her behalf, but this can't be easy for her."

"It's fine," said Kathy. "We do our best to try and keep her happy regardless."

"And I thank you for that."

Kathy looked at her watch. "Supper's not for an hour.

I'll be up front if you need anything."

"Okay, thank you." Armand gave a slight bow and walked into his mother's room.

At least she had her own space. Including a bathroom, which she was still able to use on her own, a minor miracle. It was one of the reasons Armand had been against moving her, but his two sisters had outvoted him, taking the view that making the transition too early was far better than making it too late.

He would admit that his mother's temper and short-term memory had become problematic. Armand tallied the years he himself might have left before needing assistance with the basics of living. It seemed too near for his liking. How much longer would he be able to direct the Repertory Singers? He put these thoughts out of his mind and focused on his mother.

"Hi Mama," he said. She looked over. She was reclining on her bed, fully clothed, watching a rerun of an old sitcom at low volume on the television they'd brought from her home—Armand's childhood home, which he and his sisters had sold to pay for their mother's care going forward.

"Armie," she said, frowning. "Where have you been?"

"I'm here now, Mama." Reminding her that he'd been there two days before would only turn into an argument. "How are you feeling?" He pulled a chair over from the small desk that was half-covered with family photos, including those of her four great-grandchildren.

"Like Hades," she said. "Do you know what they tried to give me for lunch today?"

"No," he said. "I did hear that you didn't eat."

"It was that...tilapia. You know I can't stand the stuff. They called it whitefish, but I could tell. By the smell."

"Don't they have alternative meals in case you don't like what's being served? It's my understanding they do."

"The smell of that tilapia took my appetite right away, Armie. They should know better by now."

"You haven't been here very long, Mama. I'm sure they'll get things figured out soon."

"What do you mean? I've been here months, haven't I? I never wanted to come here in the first place, you know."

Armand leaned back in his chair. "I know, Mama. But some things can't be avoided." Even as he said it, he felt pangs of regret.

His mother continued, "And I told Frances, and now I'm telling you, these idiot workers are always bothering me...Do this, do that. Take this, take that. They never leave me alone!"

Armand only nodded. She said, "Abandoned by my own children. Isn't it just grand? Why did I even have them in the first place? You tell me that!" She glared at him.

Armand sighed. "Frances and Emily and I love you very much, and we believe having you here is necessary for your health and safety."

"Balderdash!" she shouted.

"Please keep your voice down, Mama."

A male head peeked in. "Everything alright in here?"

"Yes, thank you," said Armand. "We were just…"

His mother cut in, "No, it's not alright! I demand to be removed from this despicable place immediately!" She tried to throw the remote control at the doorway but lost her grip, and it fell to the floor, bouncing harmlessly on the soft faux-wood floor. Armand jumped up to retrieve it, not wanting the attendant to come in the room. His mother was agitated enough already.

"We're here if you need us," said the head before disappearing.

Dottie resumed her glare. "What about your children, Armand? How would you like it if they abandoned you? You wouldn't like it at all, I can tell you."

"I don't have any children, Mama."

"Well, that's good," she said, turning toward him and putting her feet on the floor. "You won't be disappointed by their greed and selfishness." Her talk faded to mumbling. "My house…my car…my things…" She stood up.

"Where are you going, Mama?" He stood up also, half-ready to block the doorway should she make a break for it.

"Out of here," she said. "Isn't that why you're here? To take me home?"

"How about some music?" he said. "The piano is unoccupied, and I'll wager whoever's watching television out there would rather hear some of their favorite songs."

His mother's expression went from determined to uncertain. "Music?"

"Yes. I could sing some Cole Porter. Or Harold Arlen. I know how much you love Harold Arlen."

"I do love Harold Arlen. Is he here?"

"No, Mama, but you'll get the next best thing. Me!" He pointed to himself. "Let's go out to the piano." He set the remote on her nightstand.

She said, "'It's Only a Paper Moon' is one of the finest songs ever written."

"I agree. I'll begin with that." He reached for her. "Come, I'll walk you over and get you into a comfortable listening spot."

Hesitant, she took his hand. He led her in slow steps out of the room and through the hallway to the main room, where she either ignored or pretended to ignore the other goings-on. He left her standing by the bass end of the piano while he retrieved a cushioned chair from the dining area. He put it behind her and sat her down, then jogged over to Kathy at the front desk.

"Any way we could mute the television while I sing a few songs at the piano? Everyone's welcome to listen, of course."

Kathy assessed the group on the furniture. "I'm sure they won't mind."

As Armand returned to the piano and sat on the bench, Kathy went over with the remote and paused the program. The room was silent. Kathy said to those who'd been watching, "One of our guests is going to play for us a bit, and then we'll turn this back on, alright?"

"Sounds great," said one of the family members. The residents looked at Armand with curiosity.

Armand played a four-bar lead-in to "Paper Moon," noting with gratitude that the piano was more in tune than the one at the church where his choir rehearsed. He sang the song, paying special attention to his diction, and was treated to polite applause from those present. A few more residents had come out of their rooms to see what was happening.

"Now can I go home?" said Dottie.

"Mama, let's just enjoy the music for the time being, and leave discussion of everything else for later."

"Hmph," she said, her face in a scowl.

"How about another Arlen favorite?" he said. "Ah, I know." He closed his eyes and played the last eight bars of "Somewhere Over the Rainbow" as an intro. Nearing the top, he opened his eyes and looked at his mother. She was her pointing at herself. He stopped playing and tilted his head. "Are you saying you'd like to sing, Mama?"

"Yes," she said. "I would."

"Wonderful," said Armand. He played the intro again, in a different key, and she came in right on time—and on pitch—with the opening lyric:

Somewhere over the rainbow, way up high

Her voice sounded…well, old, but her intonation was good, and her words were clear. Armand closed his eyes and listened while he played. He hadn't heard his mother sing in over a decade, and it was, literally, music to his ears. He was ready to take over at the second verse, but she continued.

Somewhere over the rainbow, skies are blue

She remembered every word! Surely, he thought, she'd get tripped up by the bridge, but no—she sailed through each phrase, including the key change in the latter half.

Where troubles melt like lemon drops
Away above the chimney tops
That's where you'll find me

It was astonishing, really. It felt like a whole new beginning, causing him to reflect on his youth: His mother having been a choir director herself, there were always singers and singing around, and Armand's eventual pursuit of a career in choral arts was for certain a natural outcome of his upbringing.

Forty minutes later, Armand left his mother at one of the communal tables, picking at a serving of turkey tetrazzini. From his parked car, he dialed the older of his two younger sisters.

"Frances, it's Armand. I just left Mama."

"How was she?" said Frances.

"I think we need to reevaluate her living situation," he said. "Where we've placed her is clearly a well-run organization, but I don't think it's indicated yet."

"Armand, seriously? She's eighty-nine."

"I want you and Emily to reconsider. We can figure something out, I know we can."

"Why now? Did something happen?" ♪

The Gibson

Xavier the tenor looked at the clock on the microwave. 6:21. Dammit. He was going to be late. Significantly. And maybe late enough to miss the Gibson, which was second on the rehearsal plan. He went into the dining room to get his music. Dammit. Where had he set it? He walked through the small house until he saw the folder sitting on the desk in the bedroom. He hurried over to grab it and ran back to the kitchen. He picked up his keys from the counter and went out to the carport, where his car was parked rear-first. He got in and sped off. If he was lucky, he might walk in by 6:45.

Halfway there, he thought of his phone. He looked at the passenger seat, where it should be. Dammit! Oh, well. It wasn't that big a deal. There was crappy service at the church annex anyway.

He parked at the far end of the lot—the close spots were all taken, of course—and turned off the engine. 6:42. It was already dark. And chilly. He got out with his folder. At least there was no wind. He heard a helicopter. Then a siren.

♪ ♪ ♪

Seven minutes earlier, Dr. Tilton had finished with announcements and warmups. "Let's skip ahead to the Gibson," he said.

The altos groaned. Many of the singers—not just the altos—didn't care for the piece by Amilee Gibson due to its fast tempo and odd meter. Eleanor whispered to Katie, another soprano, "A 4/4 arrangement would be so much better."

Meanwhile, David was bothered by something else: Hal had his phone out and was staring at it, even though he'd promised to keep it off during rehearsal.

Hal said, "Whoa." He held his phone so David could see.

"Is that for real?" said David.

One of the sopranos' phones dinged. Hal said, "Looks that way."

David said, "What do we do?"

Dr. Tilton said, "Is there something I should know?"

David said, "Hal just got a..."

Hazel said, "There's an escaped convict on the loose!"

Gasps erupted. Hazel showed her neighbors. Everyone began pulling out their phones. Dr. Tilton stepped off the podium and went to get his.

"We're supposed to shelter in place," said Hal. He looked over at the door, which was propped open to let in the night air. A helicopter thwapped overhead.

Hazel said, "Lock the door! Quick!"

Theo sprang up and closed it. He said, "It locks automatically, right?"

Dr. Tilton said, "Not necessarily. You have to flip the lever."

"Flip the lever?" said Theo.

Daniel hurried over to help. He fiddled with something on the edge of the door before closing it again. "*Now* it's locked," he said.

Hazel said, "What about the windows?"

Will got up and went to the back wall. "They're all closed," he said. "I wish there were shades, though."

"Are they locked?" said Hazel.

"I think so," said Will. He leaned in close. "I can't tell for sure."

"Yes," said Daniel. "They're screwed shut."

"Is there a back door?" said Will.

Dr. Tilton said, "There's one in the kitchen. And a window, too."

Will said, "I'll check." He went down the short hall and reappeared. "Everything locked."

Dr. Tilton said, "Do we have any more information?" He and everyone else stared out the windows as the helicopter's searchlight swept across the church yard.

David read from Hal's phone over the retreating noise. "Convicted felon has escaped from custody. Exact whereabouts unknown. This individual could be armed and dangerous. All residents in the city's northwest quadrant should shelter in place until further notice."

Hal held up the phone. "They've got a picture of him," he said.

Daniel said, "We *are* in the northwest quadrant."

Theo said, "At least it's not nuclear war."

Dr. Tilton gave a soft clap. "Choir. Your attention, please."

The singers were quiet.

Dr. Tilton said, "Does anyone know the particulars of shelter in place?"

Janey said, "Will knows about lockdowns." She looked at Will.

Eleanor said, "That's right. He teaches fourth grade."

Will said, "I do know the procedure, unfortunately."

Hazel said, "I say we turn off all the lights, so we can't be seen. We're like fish in a…"

Eleanor interrupted. "How about we let Will talk? He's the one with experience."

Hazel frowned but said nothing.

Dr. Tilton said, "Will, please tell us what we should be doing."

Will said, "Hazel's right. The lights should be off."

Theo flipped both switches by the front door. The room was still partially lit by the glow of phones. Theo, Daniel, and Will made their way back to their seats.

Will said, "Phones should be off or put away. So someone outside doesn't know there's anyone here. That's why it's too bad there aren't shades on the windows."

Eleanor said, "How are we supposed to let our loved ones know we're alright?"

Georgia said, "And find out if our loved ones are alright?"

Will said, "Yeah, the thing to do is turn off all your devices. For our safety."

"I can't believe this is actually happening," said Janey.

The singers turned off their phones and tablets or switched them to silent and put them away. The room was finally dark. Secondhand light from outdoor sconces offered enough visibility to move around, once the singers' eyes adjusted.

Eleanor said, "We're supposed to be quiet, right?"

Will said, "That's right. I'm going to give a few more instructions, then we should all stay silent until we hear otherwise."

Hazel said softly, "How will we know when that happens if we can't look at our phones?"

Will said, "Somebody with good cell service should go in the closet. That person can be our contact with the outside world."

"I'll do it," said Theo. "Oh, wait, never mind. My service here isn't very good."

"Mine sucks," said Janey.

David said, "Hal has good service. And I could join him. There's room for two."

Will said, "That's fine. But try to stay quiet."

"Of course," said David. He and Hal made their way to the closet and went inside.

Dr. Tilton said in a loud whisper, "Anything else, Will?"

"No," said Will at the same volume. "I mean, we could lie flat on the floor...anyway, that's up to you all if you want to do that. The important thing is to stay away from the windows."

Several singers made space to lie down. Dr. Tilton whispered, "I'll just take a seat. Are you alright, Jackie?"

"I'm fine," said Jackie from the floor. She'd positioned herself so the piano blocked any view of her from the outside.

Will said, "I know everybody's scared, but it's going to be fine. Chances are that person will never even come near here."

Hazel said, "It's good to take precautions."

"Be quiet, Hazel," whispered Eleanor.

"I *am* quiet," whispered Hazel.

Apart from helicopters and sirens in the distance, the only sound was an irregular swishing as Mary Pat slithered along the floor from the alto section toward the basses.

♪ ♪ ♪

Xavier trotted through the parking lot and the breezeway. He came to the door of the rehearsal room. It was closed. He tried the handle. Locked. That was weird. He knocked.

♪ ♪ ♪

Every face in the choir shot toward the door. Hazel whispered, "What do we do?"

Will gave a firm "Shhhh." They waited.

The sound of someone jiggling the handle and pulling on the door was followed by more knocking.

♪ ♪ ♪

Nothing. Xavier waited longer this time for the response he was pretty sure wasn't coming. He moved away from the door and sat on a low wall. Should he go around back, to try and see through the windows? Or not bother? He thought of the Gibson. He'd worked on it a lot during the week, finally mastering the two repeating rhythms that had stymied him for months. He'd been looking forward to rehearsing that piece in particular. Being totally honest, he'd wanted to show what he could do. Dammit.

Might as well check around back. Two outdoor fixtures and a half-moon gave him plenty of light as he went. The windows were dark, as expected. Nobody was in there. He heard the helicopter again, somewhere else. More sirens. Must be a big-time traffic accident. It was scary to think about.

♪ ♪ ♪

Five minutes earlier, Will had gone to where Dr. Tilton was seated and bent down. He said in Dr. Tilton's ear, "It could be one of us. Coming late."

Dr. Tilton nodded, staring at the door. Will turned his head, and Dr. Tilton said in his ear, "I don't think we can risk it."

Will went to the closet and stepped inside. The walls, ceiling, and shelving were lit up with the blue hue of Hal's screen. There was barely enough room for the three men.

David said, "What's going on?"

"There's someone at the front door," said Will.

David and Hal looked at each other. "Shit," said Hal.

"What do we do?" said David.

Will said, "I think it might be Xavier. He sometimes comes late. If I give you his number, could you send him a text?"

"Sure," said Hal. "What is it?"

David said, "But that doesn't make sense. If Xavier's got his phone, he'll have seen the alerts."

Will thought for a moment. "You're right. Never mind. I'm going back out there. Let us know if anything changes."

David and Hal nodded.

Will exited the closet. After reporting to Dr. Tilton, he took his regular seat next to Janey. He heard angry whispering from the area of Samuel and Mary Pat, then an angrier "Shhhh!" from Eleanor.

♪ ♪ ♪

Xavier reached over the hedge and gave three firm knocks on the corner window. But for what? In case the choir was sitting there in the dark? He felt silly.

♪ ♪ ♪

The knocking on the glass startled everyone. Those who were seated, ducked. A soprano let out a low whine.

♪ ♪ ♪

Xavier went back around to the front. Maybe they were inside the church itself. Unlikely, but worth a look.

He pulled on the heavy door to the lobby. Locked. And no sign of life. He took a fast walk around the outside of the building to see if there was a side door. There was, but it was locked. Of course.

He returned to the annex. He was angry at the choir for not being where they were supposed to be, and angry at himself for not only running late but leaving without his phone. If he had it, he could text Janey or Will and find out what the hell had happened with rehearsal.

He thought again of the Gibson. Which he wouldn't get to sing tonight, ironically, now that he finally knew how it went. A passage came into his head. He played the rhythm on the door with open hands:

| ♪⁷♫⁷♫ | ♪⁷♫⁷♫ | ♪⁷♫⁷♫ |

He definitely had that one down. And by memory. Cool.

Then there was the *other* one. Could he bang that out, too? Might as well try. There was nobody around to hear, and the feel of the metal under his palms was pleasing. He counted himself in and played, mouthing the syllables:

$$|\,\sharpnote\,\gamma\,\eighthnote\,\gamma\,\twoeighths\,\gamma\,|\,\sharpnote\,\gamma\,\eighthnote\,\gamma\,\twoeighths\,\gamma\,|\,\sharpnote\,\gamma\,\eighthnote\,\gamma\,\twoeighths\,\gamma\,|\,\sharpnote\,\gamma\,\eighthnote\,$$

With zero warning, the door opened. Theo and Will grabbed Xavier by the shoulders and yanked him inside, closing the door quickly and softly behind him. Xavier started to speak, but Will placed a hand over his mouth while putting a finger up to his own. Xavier looked around the room and saw the outlines of singers seated and lying on the floor. As his eyes adjusted, he could see they were all staring at him. He nodded, and Will removed the hand.

Will motioned Xavier to follow as he went back to his seat. He pointed at several empty chairs and at the floor. Xavier gave an "OK" sign and chose a chair, still wondering what in the world was happening. What were they hiding from? Had he been in danger outside? Were they in danger now? He was considering how to get more information from Will when the closet door swung open. David leapt out and said, "They got the guy! The shelter in place is lifted!"

The singers cheered with relief and reached for their phones, then shielded their eyes when Theo switched on the lights. Those who'd been lying down returned to their chairs. Will showed Xavier his phone.

Xavier shivered. "Armed and dangerous? Whoa…"

The chatter in the room grew loud. Dr. Tilton stood up and clapped twice. "Choir! Thank you all for your cooperation. And thank Will for his leadership." The singers applauded, and Will turned red.

Dr. Tilton said, "Xavier, so glad you could join us!"

"With a little help from the Gibson," said Will.

"You scared the crap out of us," said Hazel.

Xavier said, "I am so sorry. I had no idea."

Eleanor said, "This is why it's important to be on time."

Xavier nodded but said nothing.

Dr. Tilton said, "I'm inclined to take a short break and keep on with rehearsal. What do we think?"

Theo said, "I say we work on the Gibson, while it's fresh in our minds." He laughed.

The altos booed.

Xavier raised his hand. "Can we? *Please*?" ♪

Twelve Lines

Christina's first solo—with any chorus, ever—was less than two hours away.

It had taken all of her ten years with the Repertory Singers to summon the courage to even try out for a solo. When she got the part, she was amazed. She hadn't sung the passage nearly as well during the audition as in her living room. Or the car. And other altos had performed better, she was certain. She hadn't even wanted the solo, really. She'd just wanted to prove to herself that she could face and overcome her fear. And so far, she had.

Dr. Tilton was taking the choir through a standard pre-show mini rehearsal. When they came to the Hammarstrom piece, he said, "Let's run this, and give Christina a crack at her solo." He looked at Christina. "Yes?"

"Yes," she said. She started working her way to the front.

Dr. Tilton said, "Oh, don't come out yet. Not until we get to letter C."

"Oh, right," said Christina. "I knew that." Of course she did. She'd seen how solos in the middle of pieces were handled more times than she could count. If her nerves were affecting her this much now, how would she fare in front of an audience?

Jackie played the intro. Christina came in with her section at letter A. The piece was pretty easy, actually. If only she didn't have to sing that solo.

They got to letter C, and Christina forgot to move. Dr. Tilton was gesturing for her to come forward. The other singers were looking at her. She thought she heard snickering as she laid her folder on the floor and rushed to the front. When she approached the microphone, there was a peal of feedback. Startled, she backed away. Dr. Tilton leaned over and said, "Not so close," but by then, she'd missed her entrance, so he cut off the choir. "Let's take it right at letter C," he said. He turned to Christina. "Do you know where that is?"

"Yes," she said. She'd insisted on memorizing the solo, which began at letter D, so she didn't have to hold her music while dealing with the microphone, and because she thought it presented better for the audience. More professional. It was only twelve lines, after all. But now she was wishing she had her folder. Should she ask someone to hand it to down to her? She couldn't decide.

"There's no need to be nervous," said Dr. Tilton. "Try to relax and enjoy the glory of singing."

"Okay," said Christina, sure that she looked and sounded very nervous.

Christina made it through the solo, then weaved back

to her spot in the mixed formation. Dr. Tilton stopped the choir. "That'll be fine," he said.

Fine?

Georgia caught Christina's eye and mouthed the words "Good job." Mary Pat gave a thumbs-up. Other altos sent signals of encouragement, but none of the sopranos, tenors, or basses seemed to acknowledge her at all. Was it because her performance had been subpar? She recalled instances of the whole choir applauding after a soloist's run-through. They didn't do it for everyone, though, only the singers who wowed them, and her performance apparently didn't rate. She felt a pit in her stomach. Dr. Tilton moved onto the next song.

At 2:30, the choir went downstairs to the green room. Christina joined the altos around a table. They took turns telling her how good she sounded. She wanted to believe them but knew, realistically, they were just circling the wagons. Or being kind. She wished she'd been able to practice more. She'd been afforded several run-throughs in the rehearsal room, but that was comfortable territory. Not like here, with the ringy acoustics and amplification.

She saw Dr. Tilton's hand, beckoning her. She went over. "Have a seat," he said, patting the chair next to him. Eleanor was standing on his other side, looking like she had something to say. He said, "Just a moment, please, Eleanor. I need to visit with Christina."

"Certainly," said Eleanor. She stepped just out of earshot.

"You do seem nervous," he said.

"I am," said Christina.

"You'll do wonderfully," he said. "Don't think about it too much, or you'll work yourself into a froth."

She said, "I've been singing with this group for a decade, but right now I feel like a total newbie."

"That's not a bad thing, is it?" he said. "People spend lots of money to feel new."

Christina gave a weak laugh. "Part of the problem is, I'm not convinced I deserved to get this part."

He tilted his head. "Are you questioning my judgment?"

"Well...I guess I am."

"Suit yourself," he said. "You were awarded the solo because you earned it, and if you disagree, I'm not bothered at all. I'm used to singers disagreeing with me." He pointed furtively toward Eleanor, who was turned the other way. "Understood?" he said.

Christina finally smiled. "Thank you, Armand. At this point, I just want to get it over with."

He said, "I had the same misgivings before I sang my first solo. If it makes you feel any better."

"It does," she said. "Thank you."

She went back to her seat at the table, where the altos were conversing in low tones. It seemed to Christina that they stopped talking when she approached. Did that just happen, or was her anxious mind playing tricks on her?

The first half of the concert went off without any trouble. Christina thought the group sounded quite good, actually, and Dr. Tilton seemed pleased. He told them so at intermission, during which Christina sat by herself, going over and over the solo in her head.

Midway through the second half, the time had finally come. Dr. Tilton announced to the packed house, "This next piece, by Louis Hammarstrom, features one of our altos, Christina Claussen." A few in the crowd applauded. Christina assumed it was her family and friends. (She'd already located most of the people who'd come to hear her: husband, teenaged children, parents, and three people out of the five from her work who'd promised to come.)

She focused. In minutes it would be over, one way or another. When the choir got to letter C, she made her way to the front. She stood behind the microphone, forcing a smile. And...what were the first words? She couldn't think of them. Oh, no. Her mind was completely blank. She looked at Dr. Tilton, who was busy conducting. She turned and looked at the choir. She made eye contact with Georgia in the front row, as if to say, *Help me*.

Christina turned back around to the face the audience. She still couldn't come up with her opening line. A disaster was about to unfold. Okay, not a disaster, but a missed entrance, a resulting awkward space in the music, and a lifetime of shame and regret. Okay, not a lifetime, but... this was bad. If only she'd brought her music with her. And now it was too late.

Behind and unbeknownst to Christina, Georgia held up one finger.

The choir came to letter D, and the entire alto section—spread out within the formation—dropped off their regular part and sang the first line of the solo. Oh, right! That's how it goes! Dr. Tilton showed surprise but kept on conducting.

Christina sang the second line with confidence and joy. She remembered the third line, but she had a feeling and stayed quiet. Sure enough, the altos sang the third line as a section.

Then Christina sang the fourth line, and the altos sang the fifth. Like so, they alternated through all twelve lines. Dr. Tilton must've liked it, because he was smiling ear to ear. It was the most fun Christina had ever had singing. So much fun, in fact, that she needed a reminder from Dr. Tilton to return to her spot at the end of the solo.

♪ ♪ ♪

After the concert, in the lobby of the church, no fewer than ten total strangers told Christina how much they'd enjoyed the call-and-response portion of the Hammarstrom piece—that it was a highlight of the concert. Later, in the green room, Dr. Tilton came over.

"Christina, that was brilliant! I should have known you altos were up to something."

"I had no idea, Armand. I'd forgotten the words, and they just…did it."

"Really?" he said. "Well…I think we should do the same thing at tomorrow's show. Are you willing to do that?"

"No," she said. "I'd like to sing it all myself. If you don't mind me disagreeing." ♪

Symptomatic

Samuel was in the driver's seat with the engine running. It was time to leave for the first rehearsal of the spring cycle, but Mary Pat was still inside. Damn her. He honked. The loudness of it startled him. He hoped it startled her, too. Probably not. She was probably still at the other end of the house. He honked a second time, then got out of the car and poked his head in from the garage to the laundry room. "Mary Pat! We need to go!"

No response. He shouted again. "Mary Pat!"

Still no response. He went inside and through the house to the office, where he found Mary Pat seated in front of their shared computer. "What the hell are you doing?" he said.

She looked at him. "You never paid the water bill."

"What? I did it last week."

"Well, here's a notice saying you didn't." She pointed at the screen.

"Do you have to do this right now? I'm out there in the garage like an idiot, waiting."

"I know," she said. "I heard your idiot honking. And yelling."

"You know I *hate* being late to rehearsal."

"Then you should've paid the water bill."

"Dammit, stop," he said. "You can do this when we get home."

She clicked the mouse. "All done. *Now* we won't have to worry about our water getting shut off."

"We didn't have to worry about that and you know it. Why do you have to be so difficult?"

She slid her chair back from the desk. "Time to go."

"Thank you. Jesus." Samuel hurried to the garage, assuming she was right behind him. He got in the car, and… still no Mary Pat. He looked at the clock and pressed the horn, leaning on it for several seconds, this time relishing the noise.

Mary Pat appeared with her music and water bottle and got in. Samuel grumbled as he backed the car out, closed the garage door, and started down their street.

Mary Pat said, "I had to clean up the dirty dishes you left in the sink. They attract ants."

"A couple of hours aren't going to matter," he said.

"I don't see why you can't put your dishes in the dishwasher."

"Maybe you should talk to a professional about your issue with dishes."

"Maybe *you* should talk to somebody about being a jackass," she said.

"Do you have to go there? The name-calling?"

Mary Pat raised her voice. "Do you have to honk like that when I'm the only one who makes sure the house is ready when we leave?"

Samuel shook his head and turned onto the main drag, where they rode in angry silence. Finally he said, "First of all, I *did* pay the water bill, and second of all, even if I hadn't, they send plenty of notices before they shut it off."

"You *didn't* pay it, and *I* avoided a late fee. You're welcome."

"You made us late to rehearsal," he said.

"We're not late, we're fine. But you can't ever pass up an opportunity to harass me."

"*Me* harass *you*?" he said. "This business with the dishes…talk about harassment."

"I honestly don't see why it's *so hard* for you to put your dishes in the dishwasher."

"I put my dishes in the dishwasher. I just don't do it on your schedule."

"It's not *my* schedule," she said. "It's what normal, clean people do."

"I guess I'm not a normal, clean person, then."

"I guess not." She stared straight ahead.

After a long pause, he said, "You'd think after fifty-one years, I wouldn't have to listen to this."

"You'd think after fifty-one years, I wouldn't have to ask you to put your dishes in the dishwasher."

"Maybe you married the wrong man," he said. "Do you ever think that?"

Mary Pat looked out her side window. "I do, actually."

"That's nice. Real nice. Happy half a century to you, too."

They rode another mile in silence.

Mary Pat said, "It's so easy to put your dishes in the dishwasher. That's all I'm saying."

"No," he said. "What you're saying is, you don't want to be married anymore. That's what I heard."

"Maybe you should get your hearing aids checked," she said.

"Go to hell," he said.

Mary Pat clicked on the radio, and they didn't speak the rest of the way.

Samuel pulled into the church lot and parked. Several singers had left their cars and were on their way in. Mary Pat said, "We're on time, so let's try and have a fun rehearsal, alright?"

"I'll have fun," said Samuel. "I don't know about you."

"What's that supposed to mean?"

"It means you don't know how to have fun. It's not in your DNA."

"Well then, why did you marry me in the first place?" she said.

"Good question," he said, turning off the ignition.

They got out of the car. Mary Pat closed her door hard. Samuel said, "Don't slam the door. How many times have I told you?"

"I didn't slam it," she said.

"That *was* a slam," he said. "Don't do it."

"Whatever."

They started toward the rehearsal room. Mary Pat said, "Do you have a pencil?"

Samuel stopped and looked in his folder. "Dammit, no." He turned to go back to the car.

"I grabbed one for you," she said. She held it out. "While you were sitting in the garage."

He came back and took the pencil. "Thank you."

"You're welcome," she said.

Rochelle locked her car and caught up with them. "How are you two?" she said.

"Fantastic," said Mary Pat.

"We're doing fine," said Samuel. "Thanks for asking."

After picking up their spring music, Samuel and Mary Pat went to sit with their respective sections. It would be easy to avoid eye contact.

Dr. Tilton clapped his hands. "Choir, welcome back! I trust you all enjoyed your time off." He went through the announcements and warmups, then said, "Go to the Rutter."

"Which one?" said Janey.

"Ah, yes," said Dr. Tilton. "*For the Beauty...*"

Samuel muttered to himself. He didn't like John Rutter. It wasn't that the compositions were bad, but the arrangements seemed harder—on purpose—than they needed to be. Mary Pat disagreed: She thought John Rutter had earned every ounce of his reputation as one of England's most cherished choral composers. (They'd argued over this more than a few times.)

Dr. Tilton was looking at his music. "Let me hear the..." He looked at the sopranos, then the altos. "The...the..." He stared out over the choir.

Mary Pat saw the change in Dr. Tilton's face. Samuel saw it too.

Georgia said, "Armand? Are you alright?"

His mouth was quivering. He put his hands on his music stand, as if to keep from falling.

"Something's wrong!" said Georgia. She and Katie and Eleanor leapt up from their front-row seats to help Dr. Tilton off the podium. Georgia said, "Somebody call 911!" She turned to Katie and Eleanor. "We need to get him on his side."

With Will's help, they managed to lay Dr. Tilton on the floor. Will said, "I'll get him some water."

"No, don't," said Daniel. "No food or drink. He might not be able to swallow."

"That's right," said Georgia. She was holding Dr. Tilton's head. "We need something to use as a pillow."

Rochelle pulled the cloth handbag from beneath her chair and gave it to Georgia, who arranged it carefully beneath Dr. Tilton's cheek.

Mary Pat went over. "Is he gonna be okay?" she said.

"There's no way to know, said Daniel. "The faster he gets medical care, the better chance he's got."

The noise of a siren was coming closer. Some of the choir—including Mary Pat—had crowded around the recumbent director. "Stand back, please," said Georgia. "We need space."

Daniel said, "Most of us should go home. The fewer people in here when the paramedics arrive, the better."

Samuel watched as Mary Pat backed away, crying. He felt like crying himself, but managed to ward it off. He went over to his wife. "We should leave," he said.

"Who's going to put away the chairs?" she said.

"Don't worry about the chairs."

Mary Pat wiped her eyes. "Fine, but I want us to wait outside until the paramedics are here, and we know he's okay."

"That's not helpful. We'll be in the way."

"No, we won't. I won't."

"Come on," said Samuel. He took her hand and led her out. Crossing the threshold, she pulled away. She went across the patio to a low wall and sat down. Samuel followed but remained standing.

"You go if you want," she said.

He sighed. "I'm just following the doctors' orders."

She said, "I'm not the only one. Look." She pointed to a cluster of singers who'd left the building but had stayed within sight of the door.

The ambulance arrived, its siren now off, and parked on the street. Three paramedics hopped out: two from the front with medical kits, and one from the rear with a collapsible gurney.

Samuel sat down. "I'm not leaving without you." He put his arm around her.

The paramedics disappeared inside. Mary Pat reached up and put her hand on his. "Thank you," she said. She turned her head, straining to hear whatever was going on in the rehearsal room.

Samuel said, "Something like this really puts things in perspective."

Mary Pat squeezed his hand.

He continued, "We need to show more appreciation for what we have."

Mary Pat stiffened. "I'm not sure what you mean."

"I mean...we shouldn't fight over things that don't matter. Like the dishes."

Mary Pat pushed his arm off and scooted away. "The dishes? Are you serious?"

"Yes, the dishes," he said. "Don't you see how unimportant that is? Compared to this?" He gestured at the doorway, where Dr. Tilton was being wheeled out.

Mary Pat said, "I can't believe you're still trying to win an argument."

"Uh...I think I just won."

"Whatever."

Samuel lowered his voice. "I *hate* it when you say that."

Mary Pat looked him in the eye. "You should be trying to comfort me. Instead of lecturing."

"What? I'm sitting here, aren't I?"

They watched Dr. Tilton get loaded into the ambulance. Before disappearing from view, he lifted a forearm and waved.

"That's a good sign," said Samuel.

"I hope so," said Mary Pat.

Within thirty seconds, the ambulance had pulled away. Samuel said, "*Now* can we leave?"

"You go ahead. I'll help with the chairs and get a ride with somebody else."

Samuel stood up. "You can call Georgia from the car."

"No!" said Mary Pat. The other singers looked over.

"Lower your voice," he said. "Yelling at me isn't going to help."

"I don't want to ride with you. Please go."

"Alright. Have it your way."

Samuel turned and went toward the parking lot, avoiding the other singers. Tears clouded his eyes as he crossed the blacktop. Before getting in the car, he looked to see if Mary Pat had followed. She hadn't.

He drove off, crying. Over what, exactly?

In his heart of hearts, he wasn't sure. ♪

Intermission

The Symphony Chorus

Dr. Sophia Dahl, Chorus Director

The Verdi Disaster

When Dr. Dahl reminded everyone to turn off their phones or leave them in the green room, Howard was in the john.

♪ ♪ ♪

Maestro Berloni walked onstage at Symphony Hall to enthusiastic applause. He bowed to the packed house, shook the hand of the concertmaster, and faced the orchestra. He prompted the musicians to raise their instruments. He prompted the singers to open their folders.

Howard was seconds away from his first-ever performance with a symphony chorus. He thought of his phone. He'd meant to leave it backstage, inside Lizzie's purse. But it was in his left front pocket.

He was just off center in the first row of singers, behind the percussion but on a riser. Totally exposed. If he pulled his phone out to make sure it was off, everyone would see.

Anyway, he mostly kept the ringer off. Why would it be on now? It wouldn't. Would it?

The cellos opened pianissimo. The upper strings joined in, barely audible.

Maestro cued the chorus. He'd been adamant throughout tech week that this tender first movement of the Verdi Requiem begin as softly as possible.

Howard sang, but he wasn't thinking about the music. He was thinking about checking his phone. Even if everyone saw. Better that than...it was too horrible to consider.

Seconds later, it happened. He'd recently set his ring tone to the bellow of a rutting moose. Half the orchestra and most of the chorus looked in his direction, trying to figure out where that awful noise was coming from. He couldn't wait any longer. He pulled his phone out, revealing himself. Maestro gave an angry cutoff, and the two hundred-plus musicians and singers went silent at the same time as the moose.

Maestro turned to face the audience. Howard couldn't make out what was said, but the audience was laughing. Laughing! That was a good thing, right? Howard looked to one side. The singers who'd been staring looked away.

Maestro turned back around. He pointed at Howard with his baton. "Are you ready now?" he said.

Howard's stomach turned. He put his phone back in his pocket and gave a thumbs-up. The crowd laughed. He felt sweat dripping down the back of his neck. It might be the worst moment of his life.

Maestro turned around and said something else to the audience, who cheered. Then he told the cellos, "From the beginning."

This time Howard missed his entrance. He couldn't think straight. His vision blurred. He squinted and held his folder farther away.

He was lost. Between home practice and rehearsals, he'd sung the piece more than fifty times, but this felt like sight-reading. His left-side neighbor, a kind alto with kids in preschool, saw his predicament and pointed to a measure in her music. He still couldn't get oriented. He thought he heard giggles from the crowd. He gave up and sat down.

He had to, had to, *had to* get his shit together. He counted to ten in his head. And again.

The basses sang fortissimo. It was the loud section, a choral feature. Howard flipped to the page. He could do this! He was back in the moment, and the dream was alive, with ninety minutes still to go.

He tried standing up as smoothly as possible, but his muscles had stiffened from stress and adrenaline, not to mention a long hike two days before. He felt a twinge in his left hamstring. Uh-oh.

He got leg cramps occasionally, sometimes even in public, but never in a situation like this. He had to fight it off! But there was no room. The pain became unbearable. He stepped off the riser with his good leg—mistake! The cramping muscle spasmed, propelling him forward. He landed on the side of his foot and kept falling. On instinct he stuck his arms out, flinging his folder into the air. The binder clips opened, and pages poured down. He tried spinning to avoid knocking over a suspended cymbal, but the maneuver didn't work. He hit the stand with the full force of his weight, rocketing the cymbal into the xylophone with a brutal clang. He fell to the stage between the bass drum and the timpani. He rolled onto his back and was finally able to stretch the leg. Pain, pain, pain...relief! But Maestro had given the cutoff. *Again*.

There was total silence. The timpanist helped Howard up. The kind alto asked, "Are you okay?"

"I'm fine, yeah," said Howard. He was facing the choir. Every singer looked at him in disbelief.

The voice of Maestro boomed behind him. "You!"

Against every impulse, Howard turned around. Maestro pointed with both his baton and his free hand. "Get off my stage!"

Oh, God.

He couldn't leave such a mess. He'd begun to pick up his music when Maestro screamed even louder, "Right now! *Buffone!*"

Howard felt every one of the thousands of gazes. He left the scattered pages and the toppled cymbal and the dented xylophone and slithered off between the risers and the percussion. He was careful not to touch anything. The snare drummer shook her head as he passed. He heard Maestro say something, then laughter. He made it to the wings. He heard the first bar of the piece for the third time.

All he wanted to do was get out of there. Run to his car and drive off, knowing he'd never be welcome there again. His days of singing with the symphony chorus were over—if not with any choir, anywhere, ever. This *was* the worst moment of his life.

He went to the green room for his car keys, which he'd stashed behind a chair. Why hadn't he just left his phone in the same spot? So stupid.

He heard his name. It was Dr. Dahl. They'd never spoken, except at his audition. What would she say to him now? He located his keys and sat in the chair. She came toward him. She wasn't smiling, but she didn't look angry either. She said, "You're not leaving, are you?"

"I...was planning to, yes. Why wouldn't I?"

"Come watch the rest with me," she said. "From the wings."

Howard looked confused. "I don't understand."

"What don't you understand?"

"I'm sure Maestro never wants to see my face again."

"What makes you say that?" She smiled.

"Well...he called me a *buffone*, for one. In front of everybody. I'm pretty sure that means 'buffoon.'"

Dr. Dahl laughed. "He does have a way with words."

"I made him start the piece over *twice*. At a concert. Has that ever happened? In the history of classical music?"

"Probably it has," she said.

Howard held out his hands. "So I'm sure I understand...you're saying I should...stay?"

"Stay to the end, enjoy the music, and you can apologize to Maestro afterward."

Howard looked incredulous.

"Let me ask you a question," she said. "Do you think Maestro would trade the health of a loved one for not having to restart that piece?"

"Uh...of course not, but that's..."

She interrupted. "How about the audience? Would they?"

"No, no. But..."

"That's right. And the reason is, all we're talking about here is music. It's *just music*." Howard shook his head. She said, "If I know Maestro Berloni, and I think I do, *he'll* be apologizing to *you*."

"But I took my goddamned phone onstage with the ringer on! It's...unconscionable!"

Dr. Dahl said, "And looking at it from another perspective, this audience got to witness something special."

"An idiot on display."

"No," she said. "That third first measure was the best opening to the Requiem I've ever heard."

Howard stared at her. She was beautiful. He looked down at his keys.

"Come on," she said. "We don't want to miss *Dies Irae*."

"What about the other singers? And musicians? How do I face them?"

"I guarantee you, every one of them is relieved it happened to you. And not them."

He sighed. "Okay."

She held out a hand. "You want another chance at singing with the orchestra, right?"

His eyes teared up. "Yes. I do." He took her hand and stood up.

"Make sure your phone is off." She laughed.

He made sure, then put it back behind the chair with his keys.

"Good," she said. "And remember—it's just music."

He nodded. "It's just music." ♪

Howard and the Maestro

The night of dress rehearsal for *The Bells*, Howard walked into the green room an hour before call time. Dr. Dahl was the only one there. She looked at his outfit, all black. "You didn't need to wear that tonight," she said. She was smiling.

"Yeah, I know, I just came from another gig."

"Uh-huh," she said, nodding. "What other gig?"

"I was helping out a friend with his church choir."

"That's a good story," she said.

"I realize everybody's going to think I dressed for dress rehearsal."

"Yes. We even made an announcement about it."

"I know," he said. "I was there."

"As long as your phone is off, you can wear whatever you want." She laughed.

"Ha ha, funny." He patted both front pockets. "My phone's in the car."

"Good," she said.

"Why are *you* here so early?"

"I had a gig downtown and didn't have time to go home."

"That's a good story," he said.

"I know," she said.

They smiled at each other until Howard spoke. "So... Dr. Dahl...I need to tell you, the way you treated me last season when that thing happened, the thing with the phone, and the leg cramp...that was incredible. I mean, the kindness you showed. The goodness that is in you."

She blushed. "Thank you...?"

He said, "You're exactly the kind of person, full of kindness, that I'd like to get to know better." He looked for a sign. There was none. "Therefore, I'd like to go on a date with you. If you're available for that."

"I'm sorry, I'm not." She smiled. "But thank you for asking."

"Hey, it's okay, I figured you'd be...what are the chances a beautiful and talented woman like you is single anyway? You probably have suitors lined up out front right now!" He pointed toward the lobby.

"I'm flattered," she said.

"May I ask who it is? The lucky guy?"

"You haven't heard the rumor?"

"What rumor?" he said.

"Never mind, then. No, you may not ask."

"Wait...I want to know the rumor."

Dr. Dahl smiled and shook her head.

Howard said, "I can just ask Lizzie. So I might as well hear it from you."

"Lizzie…" She sighed. "The rumor is…I'm involved with Maestro."

"Oh. Are you?"

"No, you may not ask."

Howard smiled. "I'll take that as a yes. Between you and me."

"I didn't say that."

Two female singers entered, catching Dr. Dahl's eye. "More early birds," she said.

The singers came over. Both looked at Howard. One said, "You look nice, but you didn't need to wear that tonight."

♪ ♪ ♪

The next night, Friday night, Howard was talking to the chorus manager thirty minutes before showtime. "Maestro wants to see *me*?"

"That's what he said," said Keegan. "Two minutes ago."

"I wonder why?"

"You're gonna find out, I'm sure. Follow me." Keegan took off in a fast walk, down the stairs and to the dressing area. He stopped at the door with the word "Maestro" on it. "Ready?" he said. He knocked, then put his hands behind his back and stared at the ceiling. Howard looked at the lettering on the door.

The door opened. Maestro was standing there fully tuxedoed, with only his bow tie undone. "Howard, enter," he said. He moved aside so Howard could step in.

Maestro looked at Keegan. "That is all, thank you." Keegan gave a slight bow and jogged off. Maestro closed the door. "Stand there." He gestured to a spot on the floor.

"Okay," said Howard.

Maestro started tying his tie. He talked into the mirror. "I want you to be aware of something."

"Okay," said Howard.

"It was not my decision to let you come back after the Verdi Disaster." He turned to Howard. "Did you know that is what we call it? The Verdi Disaster?"

Howard shifted his weight. "No, I didn't...know that."

"It is a good name, is it not?" Maestro was talking to the mirror again.

Howard said, "Yes, yes, it is. Very apt. Again, I am so sorry about..."

Maestro cut him off with the wave of a hand. "I am sure you will not let it happen again. My point is, it was Sophia who convinced me to let you stay."

"Oh...I didn't know that, either."

"This is why I am telling you." He resumed tying his tie.

"I'm sorry, but...why *are* you telling me?"

"Did you ask Sophia out on a date?" Maestro's eyes flicked toward Howard and back.

"Uh...I don't...know if I should answer that."

"Why not?" said Maestro.

"Well...that's my business and her business, and I don't want to share her business without her permission."

"You are a true gentleman." Maestro finished with the tie but continued to talk at the mirror, primping his hair. "Break a leg. No, I should not say that." He laughed. "Whatever you do, be sure that your phone is off."

"Yep. Phone's in the car."

Howard stood there, watching Maestro make final adjustments to his outfit. Finally Howard said, "Have a good...*you* break a leg."

Maestro didn't respond, and Howard let himself out.

That was extremely weird. And discomforting. Obviously, she told him. Because that's what people in a relationship do.

He needed to put it out of his mind. There was a concert to sing. He went back to the green room. He looked around for Dr. Dahl—Sophia—but didn't see her. Probably for the best.

He didn't want to overdo liquids, but his mouth was dry. Like he'd seen done by others, he left his music on his chair and went down the hall to the drinking fountain. Someone was filling a water bottle. They didn't acknowledge him. He waited.

It was his turn at the fountain. He moistened his mouth and swallowed only a little. Perfect.

He got back as everyone was getting seated in formation. He went to his chair. There was nothing on it. He said to his neighbor, Ted, "My music was right here." He pointed.

Ted said, "I don't remember seeing it or not seeing it."

"Have you been here? The past four minutes?"

"I've been right here since I arrived, around seven. Thereabouts."

Howard pointed again. "I left my music *right here* while I went for a drink of water."

Ted stared at the empty chair.

"And now it's *not* here," said Howard.

"Sorry, man," said Ted. "Did you ask the other guys?" He poked his chin toward the tenors on Howard's other side.

"No, but I will."

Howard tapped Victor on the shoulder. "Hey, do you know what happened to my folder? It was on my seat."

"No, sorry, haven't seen it." Victor went back to his conversation.

Howard looked under the chair and around the floor. No folder. He said to Ted, "I don't understand."

Ted said, "Somebody must've picked it up by accident. It happens. They'll figure it out when they open it. Is your name on there?"

"Yeah. I mean, I think so."

"Just be patient, it'll turn up."

Howard took a slow walk around the room, looking. If there was a folder lying somewhere, it was likely his. But he saw no such folder.

Keegan made an announcement. The singers stood up, formed lines, and left the green room for the backstage area. If Howard couldn't find a score, he couldn't sing. He ran over to Keegan.

"I can't find my score. Is there one I could use? An extra?" He was winded from the short sprint.

"Sorry, no extras," said Keegan. "Did you lose yours?"

"I guess...I don't see how. I left it on my seat, like everyone else."

Keegan looked past Howard to wave the next line onstage. Howard's row had already gone on. Was this really happening? The Verdi Disaster and now this? Some of the passing singers seemed to understand and gave either a sympathetic smile or a stone face. He had to get out of there. He headed back to the green room. Maybe Sophia was in there. Hopefully not.

He peeked in. No Sophia. He spotted a folder on a chair, on the other side of the room. Over where the tenors sat. He got closer. It was his chair. And it looked like his folder! He fast-walked the last few steps. He picked up the folder and opened it, seeing the highlighter. This was his music!

It didn't matter. The show had begun. In theory, he could...no, he'd be alone on the outside of the sopranos, with no way to blend. (Whereas if it were mixed formation, he could get away with sneaking in on the edge.)

He went to his car and drove home. He still had the Sunday matinee. People missed performances all the time, for reasons ranging from preplanned to last-minute. It wasn't the end of the world.

And then, a thought: Could it have been Keegan? The chorus manager could've picked up the folder when Ted was looking the other way. And then carried it around for a few minutes. Who would know? But he would've had to return it before directing everyone onstage. Had he had time to do that? Yes. He could've done it while the singers were standing up or just after.

But why? Why would Keegan want to sabotage his own choir?

There was only one possible explanation.

♪ ♪ ♪

It was Saturday morning, the off day. Howard had saved Dr. Dahl's number from when they'd scheduled his audition. At ten a.m. sharp, he called her.

She answered after three rings. "Hello?"

"It's Howard. Sorry to bother you on a Saturday."

"It's okay, what's up? I heard you didn't get to sing last night because you lost your music."

"Well...yes and no. My music was hidden from me and then returned when it was too late for me to go on."

"What? You think somebody did it on purpose?"

"I do. I think it was Keegan, on the orders of Maestro, who clearly doesn't want me in his choir. He told me so."

"What are you talking about?" she said.

"This is the reason for my call. I thought you'd want to know. Are you ready?"

"I am. I think."

"Okay," he said. "Last night, Keegan said Maestro wanted to see me, and he took me to Maestro's dressing room."

"This is already strange," she said.

"Yeah. So, then, Maestro told me that *A*, I was still in the choir only because of *your* personal endorsement, and *B*...he asked me if I had asked you out."

"He did not ask you that," she said.

"He absolutely did. While he was straightening his bow tie."

"What did you say?"

"I told him it was none of his business, and he let it go."

After a long silence, Sophia said, "I can't believe he did that."

"That's why I think Maestro might have put Keegan up to the little hide-the-music prank. Keegan wouldn't say no to the Maestro, would he?"

"No, he wouldn't...but what you're saying is crazy, Howard. Why would Maestro go to all that trouble? You're actually one of our better singers."

"I think..."

She interrupted, "He can say you're only in the chorus because of me, but the fact is, if you weren't good enough, you wouldn't be with us. Plain and simple."

"I appreciate that, thank you, but Maestro is clearly unhappy. He called me in to put me on the spot, and honestly it felt threatening...not physically, but psychologically. Know what I mean?"

"I'm sorry I got you involved in this," she said.

Howard laughed. "I'm the one who did the asking out. You said no."

"Uh-huh." After a pause, she said, "About the missing folder...I will ask Keegan about it. He's a bad liar, and if he hid your folder on Maestro's orders, he won't be able to keep it from me."

"Okay, thank you," said Howard. "And it seems like you agree with me that Maestro's behavior is...off. Even forgetting about the folder thing."

"Well, I won't know, really, until I talk to him. And I will. But we have a matinee tomorrow. Everything else is on hold."

"Wait, last thing," said Howard. "He told me you—as in you and him and your inner circle—call what happened last year the 'Verdi Disaster.' Is that true?"

"Yes," she said. "But it's not a bad thing. It's said with humor and affection."

"Maestro brought it up as a bad thing."

"Like I said, I need to talk to him."

Howard said, "Sorry if this disturbed you. I thought you'd want to know."

"You didn't disturb me."

"Okay, good. See you tomorrow. I'm going to crush it," he said.

She laughed and hung up.

♪ ♪ ♪

The day before, in the green room, Chelsea had knocked over her water bottle under her chair. She couldn't reach it with her free hand, so she set her music on the chair behind her. She stood the bottle up, then went to grab her folder and realized there were two that looked exactly the same. She picked up both and opened one. Ooh! Lots of yellow highlighter. She turned a few pages. It wasn't a bad idea, really. She closed the folder when she heard her name. Matilda was whisper-yelling and giving the "come here" signal. Chelsea set both folders on her chair and made her way down the row. Behind her, Howard had discovered his folder was missing and was asking Ted and Victor about it. When Keegan announced it was time to line up, Chelsea hurried to her seat and returned Howard's folder to his chair. At that moment, Howard was walking around the room, and Ted and Victor were too preoccupied with their own readiness to notice. ♪

Denied

Howard was on a hot streak: three straight concerts without a mishap. He *did* belong in the symphony chorus after all.

He grabbed the box of Frosted Flakes from the cupboard. He'd seen them at the store and been unable to resist. He'd even remembered to buy milk.

The cereal tasted so good. He hadn't eaten a bowl in years. He should do it more often. It was going to be an excellent day.

Call time was 1:15 for a 2:00 p.m. start. Howard arrived five minutes early. He saw Sophia from across the room. She looked stunning, as usual. He felt a rumble in his gut. Huh? What was that about? Then pressure on his rib cage. Uh-oh. He knew what gas felt like, and this was it. He considered what he'd eaten. Nothing since breakfa… he remembered the milk. Of course! He'd become lactose intolerant as an adult. He never thought about it because he never had occasion to drink milk. (He liked his coffee black with lots of sugar.)

Could he make a run to the pharmacy and get an over-the-counter remedy? No, there wasn't time. He'd have to clear out his system here and now. He went downstairs. The two-urinal, two-stall men's room was empty. Excellent. He chose the corner stall and took his music in with him, not wanting to let it out of his sight.

The loudness of the ensuing flatus wasn't a problem. That aspect could be controlled. But the smell...Most of his previous encounters with lactose intolerance had generated odorless gas. Not today, though, which meant he couldn't release air on stage. He'd have to hold it in. The piece was seventy minutes long.

Re-buckling his belt, he noticed it was tighter. Another bad sign, but he could do this. He had to.

♪ ♪ ♪

By the time the soloists made their last entrance, Howard was in serious pain. The pressure on his ribs was constant and, when he moved in certain ways, piercing. His stomach was distended, sticking out over his waistband. Could he make it?

They got the cue for the grand finale. Only a few minutes to go! Howard shifted his weight, and a tiny bit of air slipped out. The singers to his left and right noticed at the same time. They kept singing, but their discomfort showed.

Howard couldn't hold off any longer. His digestive system would not be denied.

During the fallout, he made faces and looked around like everyone else. The gas could have come from anyone in the area. Nobody would admit to it, and life would go on. These things happened in choirs, right?

After the last curtain call and the raising of the house lights, the chorus began to file off. There was widespread but quiet chatter. Above it rose a voice: "Nice fart, Howard!"

It was a male voice, from behind and to Howard's left. He looked back. Several faces stared at him. He said to everyone and no one, "It wasn't me." He tried to make eye contact with Lizzie, but she looked away. He was going to get blamed no matter what. That it *had* been him was the least of his problems.

In the green room, he was sure everybody was looking at him. It was so unfair! Why couldn't he get a break? And just when things were starting to feel not so precarious. Who the hell had decided to pin it on him, anyway? And why? Did he have a secret enemy in the chorus? Could it be related to the mystery of the missing and reappearing folder, which was never solved? His mind raced. He saw Ted and went over.

"Hey, Ted, do you know who said that? The 'Nice fart, Howard?'"

Ted looked confused. "Nice what?"

"Never mind. It wasn't me, by the way."

"What wasn't you?"

Howard clapped him on the back. "Good singing

with you, buddy. See you around." He saw Victor and went over.

"Hey, Victor, do you know who said that? Trying to pin that frickin' fart on me? And it *wasn't* me."

Victor shook his head. "I didn't see...I *think* I recognized the voice, but I'm not sure, so I can't say."

"Come on," said Howard. "Whoever it was should have to face me. Out in the open."

"I'm not getting involved," said Victor.

"You really won't tell me?"

"Really, I won't. Because I *don't know*. The smell *was* horrible, though. And I wasn't even that close. Assuming it was over by you."

Howard said, "Now everyone thinks I did it. And I didn't, I *swear*."

Victor shrugged. "I believe you. Sorry." He walked off.

Howard looked around for Sophia. She wasn't in the room. Good. He couldn't face her, maybe not ever again.

One of the tenors came walking up, a muscular guy with a beard. He said, "Nice fart, Howard."

Howard said, "Are you the one who said that before?"

"Yeah."

"What's your name, anyway?"

"I'm Esau. Maybe if you learned peoples' names you wouldn't be such a loner."

"I'm not a loner," said Howard. "What are you talking about?"

"Forget it, dude. The thing is, you can't drop a bomb like that during a performance. It's against the Code."

"Wait, wait!" said Howard. "What makes you think it was me?"

"Dude, because I walked into the bathroom behind you and saw you go into that stall, and you committed murder in there." Howard stared. Esau said, "I'd recognize that stench anywhere."

Howard still didn't respond. He really needed to get out of there. Esau said, "I wanted everyone to know it was you so you don't do it again. It's called shaming, and it works for all of us. No hard feelings, I hope."

Howard shook his head, dizzy with the desire to be gone. "No, it's fine."

Esau said, "I've been doing this for a long time, and that was the nastiest thing I've ever smelt onstage."

"Yeah, really sorry. Won't happen again," said Howard. "It's 'smelled,' by the way. 'Smelt' is a fish." He saw Sophia coming in and bolted for the opposite door.

♪ ♪ ♪

Sophia got up from the piano. "Good to see you." Howard and she both stuck a hand out before hugging awkwardly. "I'm so glad you decided to stay with us," she said.

"I should tell you right off the bat, I'm not staying. I wanted to tell you in person."

She furrowed her brow. "So you don't want to audition for the Mahler?"

"That's what I'm saying. Sorry for being deceptive."

"No, it's okay." She looked down at the keys. "Is it because of what happened? During the Beethoven?"

"When I broke the Code? Yeah. It's because of that."

He looked off into a corner. They were silent for ten long seconds.

Sophia said, "I think after a season you'll change your mind and come back. But by then, *I* won't be here."

"What? You're leaving?"

She nodded. "Not just the chorus, which has been amazing, but the city. I got an offer on the East Coast I couldn't refuse."

"That's great! Congratulations!" He forced himself to smile.

"Thank you," she said. "You and your adventures are one of the things I'll miss most about this job."

"Adventures?" he said. "That's a charitable way to put it." He shook his head.

Sophia said, "Since this will be my last concert cycle, why don't you stay on for me and then decide if you want to leave after?"

"For you?" he said.

"Yes. You're one of my best tenors. Best singers, period. In spite of all the breakage." She laughed, and he did too. She said, "I'm being selfish, I know."

"You are so fricking cool. And kind. But I don't think I can face these people. I'll be known as 'Nasty-Ass Howard.'"

"I doubt that. They're mostly grateful it's never happened to them."

"Nasty-ass, moose-calling, cymbal-chucking, dress-for-dress-rehearsal Howard."

She laughed. "I don't think I've heard that one."

Howard frowned. "Kind of funny, but also not."

"I'm sorry. Just trying to keep things upbeat."

"No, *I'm* sorry," he said. "I'll stop being a turd."

"Stay on with us, is my point. Consider it, at least."

"I will, and thank you for asking. Speaking of asking, how's it going with Maestro?"

"No, you may not ask," she said.

"Still that line. Alright. I assume he's not going east with you." Howard looked for a sign but saw none. "Or is he?"

She stared back at him.

"Okay," he said. "I'm going to try this one last time. Just because…I like you too much not to. Oof, here goes. Since you're leaving anyway, and your relationship status seems to be…undefined…would you consider going on a date with me? No expectations at all, beyond us hanging out together in a public place.

She smiled. "I'm sorry, Howard, the answer is no. But I do hope you'll sing in my chorus for the next four months."

Howard was quiet.

She said, "That's just on my wish list. It's whatever you decide to do."

He said, "Do you think...in an imaginary world... where I hadn't broken the Code or lost my music or the whole Verdi thing...you might have said yes? I'm saying if none of that stuff had happened."

"My answer has nothing to do with any of that," she said.

"Then what is it? You're always telling me what a great singer I am, and I'm not a bad-looking guy, so..." He trailed off.

"You're too young for me," she said. "And I'm not attracted to you in that way. Sorry."

"Oh. Okay."

"I *am* attracted to Maestro in that way. There, I said it. Now you know my secret, and I will appreciate your discretion."

"Of course," he said. "But doesn't everyone already know?"

"They didn't hear it from me," she said.

"Huh." He stared at his shoes. "Maestro turns you on... but I don't."

"I still want you in my chorus," she said. "Very much."

He looked up. "Now that I know your secret, you'll have to keep an eye on me!"

"Exactly!" She sat down at the piano. "You didn't bring the music for the audition passage, did you?"

"No, sorry."

She handed him a copy. "That's my Howard. Do the best you can," she said, and started playing. ♪

The Repertory Singers

Part II

Dr. Diana Simoneaux, Music Director

Metronome Mutiny

It was 6:30. Dr. Simoneaux tapped the bell that was clipped to her music stand. Everyone but the altos fell silent. Dr. Simoneaux tapped the bell twice more.

"Our first order of business..." She held up a postcard. The image on it was a covey of quail. "We received this from Dr. Tilton a few days ago. I'd like to read it." She cleared her throat. "Greetings, choir. I hope you're not giving Dr. Simoneaux too many fits. I know it's only been a few weeks, but I miss you already. My recovery is going swimmingly, and retirement so far suits me better than I'd hoped. I look forward to seeing and hearing you at your next concert, if not before. With song and light, Armand." Sounds of relief spread through the choir. She continued, "I'll leave this on the front table at the break. Now, let's get those voices ready."

After the warmup, Dr. Simoneaux said, "I have a surprise for you today."

Eleanor said, "We don't like surprises."

"Depends on the surprise," said Theo.

Dr. Simoneaux pointed to a narrow black tower against the side wall. "That is a Bluetooth speaker."

Katie leaned toward Eleanor and whispered, "I was wondering about that."

Eleanor whispered back, "I assumed it belonged to the church."

Dr. Simoneaux said, "Today we're going to try something most of you have probably never done in a group setting. That is, sing with a metronome."

The altos gasped. Eleanor looked at Katie and frowned.

Dr. Simoneaux said, "This choir drags, often horribly, and in my experience, metronome work can alleviate the problem."

Jackie nodded in agreement until Eleanor glared at her.

Dr. Simoneaux said, "We're giving it a go, like it or not."

Eleanor said, "Armand never made us sing with a metronome."

"I don't doubt that," said Dr. Simoneaux. "He's philosophically opposed."

Eleanor said, "Well, does he know about this?" She pointed at the speaker.

Dr. Simoneaux shook her head. "I haven't discussed it with him. Now, let's…"

Eleanor interrupted. "Why is he philosophically opposed?"

"At this moment, it doesn't matter," said Dr. Simoneaux. "Show of hands. How many of you have ever sung to a metronome with a group?"

Xavier raised his hand. "I did a few times in junior high."

Dr. Simoneaux said, "And how did you like it?"

Xavier shrugged. "I don't really remember."

"Anyone else?" said Dr. Simoneaux.

No hands went up. Eleanor said, "A metronome is a machine. It's antithetical to music. I'm sure that's why Armand wouldn't approve."

Dr. Simoneaux said, "Armand is no longer your director. I am. And my approach includes metronome work, if needed." She folded her hands. "And believe me, with this group, *it's needed*."

Eleanor tried to object, but Dr. Simoneaux tapped the bell. "Please get out the Caldwell. We'll start where it's needed most." She held up her phone. "I've got a metronome right here. It's connected to the speaker. Are we ready?"

"No," said Eleanor.

"Here we go," said Dr. Simoneaux. She tapped on her phone. A loud *thock, thock, thock* came from the speaker.

Dr. Simoneaux talked over the noise. "This is below tempo. Let's see how long you can keep up." She counted off. Jackie stayed in rhythm during the intro, but the basses fell behind as soon as they entered. By the time everyone else had come in, it was a jumbled mess.

Dr. Simoneaux stopped the metronome. "That went as expected, but don't worry, you'll get used to it." Eleanor shook her head and scowled.

On their second pass, the choir made it halfway

through page one before falling apart. Theo said, "There's something wrong with that metronome. It's speeding up." He laughed.

"It's not speeding up," said Dr. Simoneaux. "It's showing you how much you're dragging."

They went from the top three more times, making it a little farther each try.

Dr. Simoneaux said, "See? You're doing better already. I'll keep it off for the rest of tonight's rehearsal, but you can expect more of this as the season goes along." Eleanor let out a groan that Dr. Simoneaux ignored. "Because I can't stand a choir that drags, and neither can audiences."

Eleanor said, "With all due respect, Doctor, our audiences have loved us since before you could tie your shoes."

The altos looked at each other with raised eyebrows.

Dr. Simoneaux said, "The board hired me to be your music director." She was looking at Eleanor. "With Dr. Tilton's blessing." She looked away from Eleanor. "And my job is to make you sound as good, and musical, as possible." She held up her phone. "This is part of how I do it."

Eleanor said, "What if we don't agree?"

"Agree with what?" said Dr. Simoneaux.

"Singing to a metronome. I don't think any of us wants to do that." Eleanor looked around. "Am I right?"

Many of the singers nodded. "Noted," said Dr. Simoneaux. "Now, I strongly suggest for the coming week that you put in at least a few minutes of metronome work on this piece."

Eleanor said, "This is bullshit." It was loud enough for Dr. Simoneaux to have heard, but she acted as if she hadn't.

At the start of break, Eleanor, Katie, Theo, and several others went to see the postcard. Eleanor held it up. "I swear to God, if Dr. Tilton knew what just happened in here, he'd vomit up his breakfast."

Theo said, "Then we'd better not tell him." He laughed.

"There's nothing funny about this," said Eleanor.

Theo said, "She *is* our new music director, so…"

"So…if that *you-know-what*," said Eleanor, "is going to make us sing with a metronome, I'm quitting."

Katie said, "Come on, Eleanor."

Theo said, "Why don't we just see how it goes?"

"Do what you want," said Eleanor. "I'm sure there are plenty of other singers who agree with me." She set the postcard down and went outside.

After the break, Eleanor raised her hand.

"Go ahead," said Dr. Simoneaux. "But keep it short."

Eleanor said, "Some of us feel that…being forced to sing to a metronome is juvenile. And inappropriate."

Dr. Simoneaux said, "Noted. Now, let's…"

Eleanor interrupted. "We'll go to the board if we have to."

Dr. Simoneaux waved a hand. "Most of the board is here, and you're free to communicate with them. *Outside* of rehearsal."

"Maybe *I* should join the board," said Eleanor. She looked over at Daniel.

"This is not the time," said Daniel.

"Fine," said Eleanor. "But it's not musical, it's not practical, it's…not even *human*."

Dr. Simoneaux pointed at the door. "And there's the exit. Unless you're ready to quit bellyaching and sing."

Oohs came from the altos. Daniel said, "Please, Eleanor."

Eleanor stood up and gathered her things. She looked at her section. "Well?" she said.

Velma and Judith stood up and readied to leave. Eleanor waved at Katie, who was still seated. "And you?"

"Sorry," said Katie, with a shrug.

"Fine," said Eleanor.

The rest of the choir watched, mute, as Eleanor and her supporters walked out. From the patio came the sound of Eleanor's voice: "And that stupid bell! Who does she think she is?"

The altos murmured. Dr. Simoneaux said, "Not exactly a mutiny, is it? Let's go to the Portman."

♪ ♪ ♪

Eleanor's cohort showed up the following week but kept to themselves—far away from the Bluetooth speaker—until it was time to sing. After warmups, Dr. Simoneaux asked, "Who was able to put in some time with the metronome this week? On the Caldwell?"

Two dozen hands went up.

"Alright," said Dr. Simoneaux. "I want those of you who did *not* do metronome work to sing. From measure one. Stand, please." She turned to Jackie and began counting off.

Eleanor interrupted. "No metronome?"

"That's correct," said Dr. Simoneaux.

"Hallelujah," said Eleanor.

The performance was tentative and weak. After the last note, those who'd sung shook their heads and grumbled as they took their seats.

Dr. Simoneaux said, "Now, those of you who *did* work with the metronome."

It sounded like a different choir. A much better choir.

Dr. Simoneaux smiled. "I think I proved my point." She pulled out her phone. "Any further objections to me turning this on?"

Eleanor slumped her shoulders but stayed silent.

Dr. Simoneaux tapped the screen. *Thock, thock, thock* went the speaker. She counted off to Jackie, who was smiling broadly. ♪

An Alto in Need

Dr. Simoneaux didn't need to tap the bell at 6:30, because everyone was already seated and quiet, even the altos. Something wasn't right, obviously.

"Let's get those voices ready," she said on her way to the piano.

Mary Pat stood up in the alto section. "I have an announcement."

Dr. Simoneaux stopped and turned. "We're doing announcements at the break. Can it wait until then?"

"No, it can't," said Mary Pat. "Because a decision needs to be made now."

Samuel said, "I told her to wait for the break."

Mary Pat said, "I'm not waiting."

Samuel said, "You see what I have to deal with?"

Nobody moved or said anything.

Mary Pat said, "Samuel and I are splitting up."

Everyone voiced surprise except for the altos, who must've already known. Neighboring basses patted Samuel on the shoulder. Dr. Simoneaux returned to the podium and tapped the bell. "Quiet, please, singers." She turned to

Mary Pat. "I'm sorry for...what you're going through, but I don't see how it fits in with rehearsal."

Samuel said, "The break, I told her."

"Shut up, Samuel," said Mary Pat. She turned to Dr. Simoneaux. "This choir is like family to us, but we can't both stay in it. So the best thing is for the choir to choose."

Samuel said, "I suggested we take turns each concert cycle, but she didn't want to do that."

Mary Pat raised her voice. "I want to sing with my family all season. Not sit at home for five months because *he's* here." She pointed at Samuel.

Rochelle said, "Haven't you two been together for, like, fifty years?"

"Fifty-one," said Samuel.

Dr. Simoneaux tapped the bell three times, hard. Her voice had an edge. "We need to get going with warmups, alright?" She looked at Mary Pat. "Stay or go, but make up your mind." She turned to Samuel. "The same goes for you."

Samuel said, "I'm not moving. I came here to sing." He stretched out his legs.

"You're such an ass," said Mary Pat. She picked up her folder. "Fine, then. You've all made your choice for tonight. But I can tell you..." Her eyes filled with tears. "I'll be missing this with every ounce of my being!" She hurried out.

The altos stood up as if on cue. Dr. Simoneaux said, "What now?"

Georgia said, "There's an alto in need. We'll be back."

Dr. Simoneaux watched the entire alto section leave the building. She said, "How am I supposed to run a rehearsal?" She shook her head and went to the piano.

Samuel raised his hand and said, "I apologize on behalf of my wife, and for my part also."

Dr. Simoneaux said, "Thank you, Samuel. No more talking, please." She sat on the bench and took a deep breath. "Now…where were we?"

At the break, Dr. Simoneaux told the first-comers she needed to speak with Samuel. She went outside and saw him sitting alone on the farthest concrete bench. She went over.

"Samuel, can I speak with you?"

"Sure," he said. He slid over to make room. She sat.

She said, "I'm sorry you're going through this. I don't know what else to say."

"It's been a long time coming. Decades, maybe. But oh, well."

She said, "Part of my job is making sure these situations don't interrupt our preparation and performance." She paused. "We can't have blowups like that in rehearsal. We had no altos for twenty minutes."

Samuel pointed to himself. "Why are you telling me? You should be telling Mary Pat."

"I will tell Mary Pat, but right now she's not here, and you are."

"All I did tonight was show up for rehearsal, on time and prepared."

Dr. Simoneaux took a deep breath. "We'll need your cooperation in sorting this out, Samuel."

He said, "Maybe we *should* let the choir vote on it. I'll go with whatever they say, but until then, I'm coming to rehearsal. My section needs me."

"Alright, let me put it another way. If there are any further disruptions, both you and Mary Pat will be asked to step away. Is that clear?"

"Crystal," he said. "But all you're doing, really, is kicking *me* out of the choir, because the only way *she* won't cause trouble is if *I'm* not here."

Dr. Simoneaux looked confused. "Perhaps." She stood up. "At any rate, as of now, you're both welcome to stay, and I hope you do."

Samuel said, "I can't control what she does, but I promise you, I will consider all options. The fair ones."

"Alright, Samuel."

"Thank you, Dr. Simoneaux, and…I was…well, I'll go ahead and tell you. Mary Pat says you don't hold a candle to Dr. Tilton, but I disagree. I think you're a much better music director."

"I'd prefer you not put words in Mary Pat's mouth."

Samuel waved his hands. "You're right, you're right. Forget I said it."

"Agreed. I'll see you in a few minutes."

She went back inside, where some of the singers were going toward their seats. She saw the altos—still without Mary Pat—huddled off to the side. She tapped the bell.

"We're going to skip announcements today, because of the late start. Unless anyone has something that is both relevant and urgent."

Georgia stood up. "The alto section thinks the choir should vote for who they want to stay this cycle, Mary Pat or Samuel."

Samuel said, "I wonder who *you're* all gonna vote for."

Dr. Simoneaux tapped the bell three times. "Enough!" She looked at Samuel. "I'm sorry, Samuel, but I have to ask you to leave. This is too disruptive."

"You got it, teach," said Samuel. He stood up with his folder.

Dr. Simoneaux said, "I prefer to be addressed as 'Dr. Simoneaux.' Not 'teach.'"

"Yeah, sorry," he said. He turned and walked out.

Dr. Simoneaux said, "Rehearsal is for rehearsing. Are we clear? Now, please get out the Whitacre." She opened her folder. Without looking up, she said, "Georgia, take your seat."

Georgia said quickly, "Singers, there's a vote right after rehearsal." She gave Dr. Simoneaux a deferential wave and sat down. "No more, I promise."

"I hope that's the case," said Dr. Simoneaux. "Now, let's have the altos at measure forty-five."

It was 9:00 on the dot when Dr. Simoneaux gave the last cutoff of the evening. She said, "Regarding this vote business, do what you please, but understand that roster decisions are mine alone. Also, make sure the door is locked when you leave." She shunned attempts to speak with her as she hurried out.

Georgia said to the group, "Let's have that vote."

Daniel said, "Georgia, I don't think this is a good idea."

"Leave if you want," said Georgia. "Those of us who want to vote are going to stay."

"Alright," said Daniel. He left, and around half the choir went with him.

Georgia said, "It should be secret ballot. Does anyone have paper?"

Theo said, "We're mostly altos here. Of course Mary Pat is gonna win."

Georgia said, "If the basses wanted Samuel to win, more of them should've stayed."

Will said, "You think Dr. Simoneaux gives two shits about a vote?"

Theo said, "This is moronic," and exited.

Rochelle said, "Does anyone know what happened with Mary Pat and Samuel? After all this time?"

Georgia said, "What difference does it make? We're voting on who we'd rather sing with."

Rochelle said, "I don't know, it might matter. If we find out, you know, that one of them did something...*you know.*"

Georgia said, "I suggest you mind your own business. I'll go find paper."

Janey, the only other tenor who'd stayed, raised her hand. "Wait...I want to share my vote now. My vote is that they both stay."

Will raised his hand. "I vote that, too."

Georgia said, "You can't do that. You vote for Mary Pat or Samuel. Or you abstain."

Katie raised her hand. "I vote for both."

Hazel raised her hand. "Forget the secret ballot. I vote both."

Georgia said, "But that's not…" She was interrupted by more hands going up. She said, "Forget it all, then. If you won't do it right." She turned to her section. "Time to go home."

♪ ♪ ♪

The following week, neither Mary Pat nor Samuel was in attendance. The altos were even more somber than the week before. At 6:30, Dr. Simoneaux tapped the bell. She said, "I keep wanting to save announcements for the break, but it never seems to work out." She took a deep breath. "And so…I need to announce that after discussions with the board, I've decided to suspend both Mary Pat and Samuel for the remainder of the cycle." The altos gasped louder than everyone else. Dr. Simoneaux said, "After the concerts, I will reevaluate."

Will leaned over to Janey and whispered, "Hardcore."

Georgia stood up. "That doesn't seem right, Dr. Simoneaux. You know how much this choir means to Mary Pat."

Dr. Simoneaux said, "I have been in touch with both Mary Pat and Samuel."

Georgia spoke louder. "Did you hear me? This choir means too much to Mary Pat. Especially right now."

Dr. Simoneaux stared at Georgia. "Perhaps," she said, "that is part of the problem."

Georgia started to speak, but stopped. She sat down in a daze.

Dr. Simoneaux said, "Now, let's get those voices ready." ♪

The App

It was Janey who got the app first. Where she got it, or from whom, she never said. Before rehearsal, she shared it with Will and then Georgia, who shared it with the other altos. Will shared it with Theo, because, how could he not? And Theo shared it with as many singers as possible.

Even the usual busybodies were buried in their phones at the break. Dr. Simoneaux was relishing the respite until Gretchen came up. Gretchen said, "Do you know about the app?"

"App?" said Dr. Simoneaux. She looked like she wished Gretchen would go away.

Gretchen said, "It's called 'Rank My Choir' and it's this app where you rank the people in your choir by singing ability."

Dr. Simoneaux said, "I'm sorry, Gretchen, I'm just..."

"Let me show you," said Gretchen. "It'll be easier than trying to explain." She held out her phone for Dr. Simoneaux to see.

Dr. Simoneaux stared at it. "That's our current roster," she said.

"Yeah," Gretchen said. "From one to forty-five. Look at the order." She waited as Dr. Simoneaux leaned in closer.

Dr. Simoneaux said, "Who's doing the ranking?"

Gretchen said, "The members of this choir. Who else?"

Dr. Simoneaux said, "Indeed."

"Yeah, look," said Gretchen. She pointed to the lower left-hand corner of the screen. "Twenty-nine submitted so far."

"My God, that's a lot."

"Well, think about it," said Gretchen. "If everyone else is doing it, then by not doing it, you're at a disadvantage."

"If you care about some silly app."

"Right, of course," said Gretchen. "Which nobody does, really. I don't think." She closed the app on her phone. "I was just wondering if you knew, that's all."

Dr. Simoneaux said, "Where did they get our roster?"

"From our website."

"Interesting," said Dr. Simoneaux. "Did you do it?"

"Do what?"

"Rank your choir?"

Gretchen put her phone in her pocket. "Me? No, I just downloaded the app so I could see what everybody was talking about. I didn't actually *do* it. No." She walked off, shaking her head.

After the break, when Dr. Simoneaux asked if there were any announcements, Hazel stood up. A few singers instinctively looked away, including Gretchen. Hazel said,

"I have something. I want to announce that I am hurt and offended at being the lowest-ranked singer in this choir."

Nobody said anything.

Hazel said, "If you're all going to say I'm the worst, I should at least know why. So I can work on whatever it is."

Dr. Simoneaux was looking around. Hazel said, "Dr. Simoneaux, I'm sorry to take up rehearsal time for this—you'll probably tell me to shut up and sing—but I think I deserve to know who ranked me last."

"Go ahead," said Dr. Simoneaux.

"Really?" said Hazel.

"Really," said Dr. Simoneaux. She turned to Jackie. "We'll get going soon."

"No problem," said Jackie.

Hazel looked out over the choir. "Okay, so…who put me last? Raise your hand."

No hands went up. The altos exchanged glances.

Hazel said, "Let me see…" She looked at her phone. "Thirty-six of you filled out a ranking and none of you put me last?" She paused. "Then…how did I end up there?"

The altos shifted in their seats.

"Come on, now," said Hazel. "Not one of you is willing to admit it?"

Philip said, "I'm second to last."

Hazel said, "Then you know how I feel."

Xavier said, "I'm third to last. And I did submit a ranking. But I didn't put you last, Hazel. I swear."

"Where did you put me?" said Hazel.

"I don't remember, honestly. I just know it wasn't last."

Eleanor said, "Who *did* you rank last, Xavier?"

Xavier stared at her. "I'm done talking about this," he said.

Katie raised her hand and said, "I put you last, Hazel. I'm sorry. Somebody had to be last. It doesn't mean you don't belong in this choir."

Hazel said, "Thanks for your honesty, Katie. You're the only singer here with any balls."

Theo raised his hand. "I ranked you last," he said.

Janey and Will raised their hands. "We did too," said Janey. "It was nothing personal."

The altos raised their hands all at once. Georgia said, "We still like you, Hazel."

More hands went up around the room. Hazel said, "Dr. Simoneaux, may I keep going? This is very helpful to me."

"By all means," said Dr. Simoneaux. She raised her eyebrows at Jackie before crossing her arms and resting on her back foot.

"Thank you," said Hazel. She addressed the group. "Now that we're being honest, maybe somebody can tell me what it is about my singing that makes me *the worst singer in the whole choir*." She looked at Katie. "Katie?"

Katie said, "You're loud."

Hazel said, "Well...Dr. Simoneaux doesn't tell me I'm loud." She looked at Dr. Simoneaux, who showed no reaction.

"Dr. Simoneaux doesn't have to sit right in front of you," said Katie.

"Ouch," said Theo.

Katie said, "You said you wanted honesty."

Hazel said, "Thank you, Katie, I appreciate that."

Georgia said, "You hold your esses. We can hear it from over here."

Hazel said, "Okay, I've worked on that a lot, so it's not me you're hearing."

Eleanor said, "It's you."

Janey said, "It's definitely you, Hazel. Sorry."

Hazel said, "Okay then…at least my tuning is good, right? I'm not pitchy or anything?"

The room was silent. Finally Katie said, "Sometimes when you're really loud, you can be a little off. But your tuning is good most of the time, for sure."

Hazel was stoic. Dr. Simoneaux said, "Is there anything else, Hazel?"

"No," she said. "I guess…well, do *you* think I'm loud, Dr. Simoneaux?"

"What I think is irrelevant. But yes, you are loud."

"Too loud?" said Hazel.

"Often, yes."

"Then why haven't you said so?"

Dr. Simoneaux folded her hands. "When I say things like, 'Singers, you're too loud,' I'm not talking to *all* singers. I'm talking to the singers who are too loud. And you're not the only one."

Will raised a hand. "I can be too loud also."

Dr. Simoneaux gestured at Will. "For example. Or when I say, 'Don't hold onto those esses,' I'm not talking to *all* singers. Just those who need the correction."

Hazel said, "Oh." Her eyes teared up. "I guess this means...I really *am* the worst." She looked down at her feet.

Dr. Simoneaux said, "If you don't like how your peers rated you, my suggestion is to work harder and get better. I'm sure you can move up the list over time."

"What?" said Eleanor. "That's your response?"

Dr. Simoneaux said, "Do I need to say it again?"

Eleanor stood up with her folder and her purse. "This is not fun anymore. Not like it was. I'm sorry, everyone." She headed for the door. Passing Hazel, she said, "Should I wait for you?"

Hazel said quietly, "I want to stay."

"Alright," said Eleanor. She turned and spoke to the whole choir. "A line has to be drawn somewhere." She walked out.

Half the sopranos started gathering their things. Dr. Simoneaux said, "Here we go again." She shook her head at Jackie.

Marnie whispered to Susannah, "What do you think?"

Susannah whispered, "I have a ton of stuff to do tonight. And if this many people are leaving..."

They nodded at each other and joined the exodus. As did Gretchen and Rochelle.

After a brief huddle with her section, Georgia stood up. "We're embarrassed by the whole situation and our part in it. So we don't think we can continue with rehearsal tonight."

The altos went out together as Dr. Simoneaux watched, her arms crossed in a show of defiance. "Anyone else?" she said.

Daniel said, "I think we might have a larger problem here."

Dr. Simoneaux said, "Noted. But for now, rehearsal is officially canceled. We'll try again next week." She turned to Jackie. "Sorry, Jackie." She looked at Hazel. "Hazel, will you please stay after for a moment?"

Hazel nodded. The remaining singers put the chairs away and filed out. A few patted Hazel on the back or offered words of encouragement.

When everyone had left, Dr. Simoneaux retrieved a chair and sat facing Hazel. She said, "I'm sorry if what I said sounded harsh, but I don't see that it does anyone any good to hear varnished truth."

Hazel started to cry. "It's not you, it's…that they all agree I'm the worst. Or most of them." She cried harder. Dr. Simoneaux reached out and put a hand on her shoulder. Hazel said, "I work on this stuff a lot! I don't understand."

Dr. Simoneaux said, "I can see how that would be frustrating." She pulled back her hand.

Hazel said, "Can I ask you an honest question? I mean, can you answer it honestly?"

"I can try."

"You inherited this roster. The one we have now."

"That's right," said Dr. Simoneaux.

"Right...so, if I wasn't on the roster, and I came in to audition today, would I make it? That's the question."

"It would depend on our needs, of course, and..."

Hazel interrupted. "Assume you need a soprano. You need a soprano, and I walk in the door. Do I get the spot?"

Dr. Simoneaux was thinking. Hazel said, "No varnished truth, remember?"

Dr. Simoneaux sighed. "Probably you would not. You've got too many areas that need improvement."

"I thought so." Hazel sank down in her chair. "This is why half the time I don't feel like I belong. Or most of the time."

Dr. Simoneaux didn't respond.

Hazel said, "So...I should just quit, right? I've taken voice lessons, I've tried video tutorials, I've even done metronome work! Nothing helps."

Dr. Simoneaux looked at her phone. "We've got a half-hour of rehearsal time left. How about you and I go over some things at the piano?"

Hazel wiped her eyes. "Yeah. I'd like that. Except, I'll be embarrassed at how bad I am."

"Nonsense. You're a singer in my choir, and it's my job to help you sound your best."

Hazel laughed a little. "I guess we're stuck with each other."

Dr. Simoneaux smiled. "It would appear so."

♪ ♪ ♪

Three days later, Eleanor had just put an upside-down cake in the oven when her phone rang. It was Daniel.

"Hello, Daniel," she said. "I'm anxious to hear what you have to say."

"Well, you might not like this, but…the board is not taking any action at this time, beyond acknowledging your concerns."

"*My* concerns?" she said. "It's not just me."

"You are correct, it's not just you. There have been a number of communications."

"Cut the board-speak, Daniel. At least tell me there's going to be some kind of reprimand. The way she treated Hazel at the last rehearsal, in front of everyone, was unacceptable."

Daniel said, "I've spoken with Dr. Simoneaux, as have other board members, and that's all that's going to happen for now."

"Mm-hm," said Eleanor. "I guess I'm not surprised. But let me say, for the record, that our music director is not doing her job. The way she should."

"You're already on the record as having articulated that."

"Well, put it on the record again," she said.

"Alright, Eleanor. But you have to be realistic about what can and can't be done at present."

"Oh, I am. Thank you. I'm curious, though, has Armand been informed?"

"Absolutely not." Daniel's voice was stern. "That would be totally inappropriate, especially considering his condition. I hope you haven't tried to involve him."

"I haven't. I was just wondering."

After a pause, Daniel said, "I spoke with Hazel, and she seems satisfied with how the situation turned out."

"I spoke with Hazel, too. Multiple times."

"And? Did she express the same sentiment to you?"

"I don't want to go into what was said between Hazel and me."

"Alright, that's fine," said Daniel. "But the fact remains…and this is coming from the board, not just me… we can't have our section leaders getting up and walking out of rehearsal. We just can't have it. So I'd like assurances from you that between now and the end of the cycle, you'll be able to…manage your feelings."

"My feelings are managed fine. Did you talk to Georgia? What did she say about all this?"

"Georgia assured me that she'll stay focused on the music and on the upcoming concerts. And we need the same from you. Please."

Eleanor was silent.

Daniel said, "I'm asking as a longtime colleague and friend."

Eleanor sighed. "You have my word, Daniel. But I need to have yours that all of this will be reviewed."

"Yes, it will. We give our music director a performance review each off-season as a matter of course. And everything we've talked about will be part of those discussions."

"Thank you," she said. "That's what I wanted to hear."

"I'm glad. And thank *you* for everything *you* do. I don't want it to get lost that we value your enormous contributions to this organization."

"You're welcome, Daniel. I'll see you at rehearsal."

"Goodbye, Eleanor," he said, but she'd already ended the call. ♪

Soprano Bond

Two weeks after the kerfuffle over the app, Eleanor pulled out of the church parking lot and drove slowly north. Another singer had pulled out behind her—she couldn't see who in the dark—but it didn't matter. Instead of making her usual right turn at the end of the street, she went left. The car behind her went right. Excellent. She was now free to double back undetected.

She parked on the street, two houses down from the annex, just close enough to see Dr. Simoneaux's compact hatchback. It was 9:09. Dr. Simoneaux would be locking the rehearsal room doors about then.

A minute later, the director appeared, carrying her tablet, the Bluetooth speaker, and a stand. She unlocked her car and got in. When she pulled out onto the street, Eleanor followed.

Where would Dr. Simoneaux go? Home, most likely, wherever that was. In any case, Eleanor was going to find out. She'd already told her husband to expect her later than usual—that the sopranos were holding a sectional after rehearsal to iron out a few rough spots. After that, they might go for a drink.

Whereas Armand had hosted events for the choir at his home, nobody knew anything about the living situation of his replacement (if you could call her that). She'd moved back here for the job, hadn't she? Yet, to Eleanor's knowledge, Dr. Simoneaux had never asked any of the singers for guidance on local restaurants, entertainment, or anything else. As if she wanted nothing to do with the choir outside of her official capacity.

Dr. Simoneaux drove slowly. She was probably talking on the phone, which wouldn't be a surprise. The woman seemed to care only about herself and what *she* wanted. She took what Eleanor called a "my way or the highway" approach to directing, which in Eleanor's opinion was not at all appropriate for an all-volunteer, audition choir.

The hatchback's right turn signal flashed in the middle of the block. Huh? The brake lights flared, and Dr. Simoneaux pulled into the parking lot of…the Lazy Nickel?

Eleanor slowed as she passed. Dr. Simoneaux went straight into a parking space. Most likely, she'd gotten so involved in her phone call that she'd needed to pull over. What she should've done from the beginning.

Eleanor sped around the block, rolling through two stop signs to get back to the bar as quickly as possible. When she approached it the second time, she saw that not only was the hatchback still there, but its lights were off. By the glow of the bar's neon sign, Eleanor could see that the driver's seat was empty. What was going on? Had Dr. Simoneaux gone inside the sleazy establishment?

Eleanor went around again, this time slower. If the director was indeed inside, there was no rush. The question now: What next?

Eleanor *should* forget the whole thing and go home, but she couldn't. This was too odd, too potentially juicy, to leave uninvestigated. She pulled into the lot and parked at the far end. She turned off the engine. Should she go inside? She almost had to. But she'd need to be sly about it.

She got out and looked around. The front door of the bar started to swing open, and she ducked. Peering over the roof of her car, she saw that it wasn't Dr. Simoneaux. Good. She crept toward the entrance. She could half-open the door, take a quick scan of the inside, and leave. Either she'd see what Dr. Simoneaux was up to or she wouldn't.

Eleanor turned her back as another patron came out, this one staggering drunk—and hopefully not on his way to operating a motor vehicle. She felt exposed under the dingy light. It was time to act or go home.

She pulled open the door. The interior wasn't as dark as she'd expected, and the recorded music was set at a reasonable volume, but the place smelled like dirty dishrags. She checked the tables, then the long bar that stretched from the entrance to the rear of the room. In the center of it, seated alone, with a drink in front of her, was Dr. Simoneaux. And she was staring right at Eleanor.

Eleanor stared back like a deer in headlights. She finally released the door and came all the way inside. Dr. Simoneaux waved, then beckoned her over. Eleanor had no choice but to comply.

"What are you doing here?" said Dr. Simoneaux.

"What are *you* doing here?" said Eleanor.

Dr. Simoneaux held up her glass. "I'm having a drink. And you?"

Eleanor stammered "I was…um…"

Dr. Simoneaux waited as Eleanor struggled to come up with an answer, then said, "You followed me here."

"What?" Eleanor's face flushed with heat.

"I know because I saw you parked on the street when I left the church."

"Oh…okay." Eleanor thought about running for the exit.

Dr. Simoneaux pulled out the stool next to her. "Have a seat," she said. "It seems we've got some things to talk about."

"Things…?"

"You shouldn't spy on people. It's sneaky and dishonest."

Eleanor shook her head. "I wasn't."

"Come on, Eleanor. Have a drink with me. I'm buying."

Eleanor stared at the stool. The bartender came over. "What can I get you?" he said.

"Nothing for me," said Eleanor. "Thanks."

The bartender said, "If you change your mind, lemme know."

Eleanor nodded and sat. Dr. Simoneaux said, "You're probably wondering why someone like me would hang out in a place like this."

"Well…yeah."

"I'm unlikely to run into anyone I know," said Dr. Simoneaux. She looked around the room, then reestablished eye contact. "Except for a certain nosy soprano who's had it in for me from the beginning."

"Had it in for you? That is not…no."

"Not at all?" said Dr. Simoneaux. "Not even a little?" She laughed.

Eleanor's face flushed again. She didn't know how to respond. Finally she said, "Are we so hard to direct that you need alcohol after?"

"Not always," said Dr. Simoneaux. "But sometimes."

"Why not just drink at home? I still don't see why…here."

"I make it a rule never to drink alone." She took a sip.

"Aren't you drinking alone right now?"

Dr. Simoneaux said, "There're a dozen people here at least, plus Mikey behind the bar is an excellent conversationalist."

Eleanor was gaining confidence. "Well, I'd say anyone who comes in here on a Tuesday night is probably an alcoholic."

"Does that include you?"

"I'm not drinking."

"Not yet." Dr. Simoneaux took another sip.

"What does that mean?"

Dr. Simoneaux smiled. "I could offer you a glass of wine at my place, but it's small."

"I'm sure it's more comfortable than here," said Eleanor.

"It's a one-bedroom apartment, a second-floor walk-up. There's a balcony with room for zero chairs."

"Oh," said Eleanor.

"It's all I can afford while I get back on my feet financially."

"Did something happen?"

"If I'm going to tell you my life story, it should be over a drink."

Eleanor considered it. She said, "I already know you got your degrees in Utah, and you've known Dr. Tilton since you were in high school, when he directed you as lead first soprano in the All-State Choir."

"Those are the parts everybody knows. I'm talking about the *real* story."

Eleanor considered further. "What are *you* having?" she said.

"Club soda with lime. But I'd be happy to order us both something stronger if you want to stay."

"And here I thought you were *drinking* drinking. I apologize."

Dr. Simoneaux raised her eyebrows. "I know how to *drink* drink, but I need to be fully aware when I'm being tailed by one of my singers."

"I see your point," said Eleanor.

"I'm assuming nobody knows about your espionage, nor do they need to. It can stay between us." She offered a handshake. "Soprano bond."

Eleanor accepted the handshake. "Soprano bond." She smiled and pointed at the bartender. "Mikey is his name?"

"That's what he claims. I've only just met him." Dr. Simoneaux laughed.

Eleanor said, "You've never been here before, have you?"

"Would you have followed me into a nicer place?"

"Maybe," said Eleanor.

"But when I walked into the Lazy Nickel, you couldn't resist."

"Very clever, you are. And the best part is, I'm not lying to my husband."

"Pardon me?"

"I'll explain in a minute." Eleanor looked down the bar and raised a hand. "Mikey? I think I've changed my mind." ♪

A New Tenor

It was Howard's turn to sing. The four basses and one alto who'd gone before him had done fine—especially the alto—but none were as good as he was at his best. Of this, he was certain.

He made sure he was relaxed. And breathing. He nailed the entrance. The rest flowed as naturally as a stream.

"Wow," said. Dr. Simoneaux. "Very impressive. And beautiful."

The other aspiring soloists nodded and added words of appreciation, but Howard knew: On the inside, they were jealous. Dr. Simoneaux hadn't been so complimentary of anyone else. Nor was she complimentary at all of the last singer, David, who in Howard's opinion should not have auditioned.

Dr. Simoneaux said, "Thank you all. I'll give you my decision at the next rehearsal."

The group disbanded. Howard went to the drinking fountain. On the way back to his chair, he passed by Xavier. Howard was expecting congratulations, but instead he got what felt like a cold shoulder. Huh? No, it couldn't be. It must be his imagination. He went and sat down. He turned around to face Will, with whom he'd become somewhat friendly.

"I think I got a shot," said Howard. He waited for Will to agree, but Will instead opened his folder and started looking at his music. "Will?"

"Yes?" said Will, without looking up.

"Did you hear what I said? Sorry."

Will looked up. "I heard you. You think you've got a shot at that solo." He looked back at his music.

"Yeah, okay," said Howard. He turned to face the front. Break was ending anyway. But he was nagged...had Will just given him the cold shoulder, too? Or was that also his imagination?

It was midway through the second half of rehearsal when the thought occurred to Howard that maybe he'd done something wrong. The basses—not all of them, but enough to be significant—were giving him periodic unfriendly glances. Could it have something to do with the solo audition? A theory began to form in his mind.

Dr. Simoneaux ended rehearsal with a short but stern lecture about the importance of home practice. As soon as she released the group, Howard turned around to talk to Will.

Will said, "Hold on a sec," and got up.

Howard looked at Janey. "Did I do something wrong?"

Janey said, "If you ask me, no. But I'm not someone who cares about the Code."

Howard felt a stab of fear. He'd known there was a chance, if not a likelihood, that his gassy faux pas with the symphony chorus would follow him to the Repertory Singers, but why tonight? In his third rehearsal? He looked Janey in the eye. "I did not break the Code tonight. I swear to God."

She said, "Not like you did at Symphony Hall, no. *Thank* God." She laughed.

Howard said, "What are you talking about?" There was nothing funny about this.

Janey stood up. "I need to get to Rochelle's and let her dogs out. If I were you, I'd talk to Elroy."

"Elroy?" said Howard. He looked over at the elderly tenor who was seated in the back row, organizing his notes. "Because he's our section leader?"

Janey nodded. "That...and, he's an authority on the Code." Howard started to say something, but Janey held up her hand. "I really gotta go. Text me tomorrow if you want, but for now, get with Elroy."

"Yeah, okay," said Howard. "Thanks."

He looked around. Half the singers were already gone. His eyes met those of David, the weakest of the solo hopefuls. Howard smiled and waved, but David looked away and whispered something in Hal's ear. Hal shot Howard a nasty glare before taking David's hand and leading him out the door.

Now the only singers who remained were a few sopranos, Howard, and Elroy. Dr. Simoneaux and Jackie were talking at the piano. Howard went and sat down next to Elroy. "Elroy?" he said. "Do you have a minute?"

Elroy smiled. "For a tenor? Always."

Howard said, "I don't even know what I'm asking, actually...I just...apparently I did something wrong tonight."

Elroy said, "You sure did, sonny. You broke the Code."

Howard threw up his hands in frustration, dropping his music folder in the process. "What the hell did I do?" he said.

"Easy now," said Elroy. He pointed at Dr. Simoneaux. "I have something to go over with our director, then we can visit. How does that sound?"

"So...here?" said Howard. He picked up his folder.

Elroy said, "Yep. Sit tight, and I'll be right back with you."

"Okay," said Howard.

"We'll get it sorted out," said Elroy. He went to talk to Dr. Simoneaux.

As Howard waited, he searched on his phone for the Code. He tried all manner of wording, but the closest he could come up with were official codes of conduct for individual choirs or organizations. Nothing along the lines of the "Code" he had now violated more than once. He kept searching until he heard the door pull shut. He looked up and saw he was alone with Elroy.

"Alright," said Elroy. He placed one of the few remaining chairs next to Howard. "What is it you want to know?"

Howard looked at him. Hadn't he already made that clear? He said it again. "What did I do tonight to break the Code? And what is the goddamn Code, anyway?" He held up his phone. "I can't find anything about it online, not even a reference to it."

"Whoa, sonny. Losing your temper won't accomplish a thing."

Howard said, "Oh, is losing my temper breaking the Code, too?" He laughed without smiling.

"No, no," said Elroy. "And that's a good place to start. What's *not* part of the Code."

"I don't understand," said Howard.

"Going after another singer's better half," said Elroy. "You think that's part of the code?"

"What? How should I know?"

"Well, it's not," said Elroy.

"It sure as shit should be."

Elroy laughed. "You'll never understand the Code with that attitude."

Howard let his arms fall to his sides, limp. "Could you please just explain it to me, then? Specifically, what I did *tonight*?"

Elroy took a deep breath. "You tried to take a solo that belongs to a bass."

"I thought that might be it!" said Howard. "The BS started right after my audition. Which I crushed, by the way."

"I know, I heard it. And that made things worse."

"Okay, then...what do I do?"

"There's nothing you *can* do," said Elroy. "The thing about the Code is, there's no putting the turd back inside the goose, as they say."

"So..."

"You accept it and move on. Like everyone else. It won't ruin you forever."

Howard said, "Why can't I just email Dr. Simoneaux and remove myself from consideration?"

"You're not listening, sonny. It doesn't matter if you get the solo or not. The deed is done."

"You're saying I broke the Code just by auditioning?"

"Yep. You did."

Howard thought for a moment. "An alto tried out, too. Why didn't she break the Code? Or did she?"

Elroy said, "It's not complicated, sonny. This part of the Code is between tenors and basses. And altos and sopranos. If you follow."

"So...an alto can go for a bass or a tenor solo, but not a soprano solo."

Elroy patted Howard's leg. "You got it."

Howard stared blankly. This made very little sense. He said, "Is there anything else? Besides this solo thing and farting during a concert?"

Elroy shook his head. "Nope, that's it. And from what I hear, you done 'em both."

"How was I supposed to know? I mean, about the solo audition."

Elroy looked him in the eye. "You're telling me it never crossed your mind that those basses might be ticked off seeing you over there?"

"Well, yeah, it crossed my mind. But why didn't anyone say anything? Why didn't Dr. Simoneaux? She knows the Code, right?"

"Directors don't get involved in this stuff. They've got other things to think about. Especially this one. The choir's been putting her through her paces, as they say."

Howard held up a finger. "What about telling somebody they're off-pitch? That's not a…violation?"

"Nope," said Elroy.

"Okay…how about…reporting someone who's singing something wrong to the director. That *has* to be a no-go."

"Perfectly fine."

"Hiding somebody's music?"

"Nope. And why in the world would you want to do that?"

"Never mind, long story," said Howard. "What about dating the music director?"

Elroy squinted. "Are you looking to woo Miss Diana?"

"No, no. But if I was?"

"Fine," said Elroy. "Woo to your heart's content."

Howard said, "But…" He wrung his hands.

"It'll sink in eventually," said Elroy. He looked at his wristwatch. "I'd best be going now. It's getting near my bedtime."

"Wait, last question," said Howard. "Is this Code written down somewhere? Anywhere?"

"Not that I know of," said Elroy. Howard wanted further explanation, but Elroy stood up. "Let's go. It'll be alright, I promise."

Howard stood up. "I sure hope so. I practically just got here, and everybody's pissed at me. Maybe I should quit."

Elroy said, "Don't do that, sonny. As leader of the tenor section, I'd hate to lose you."

As advised, Howard did nothing over the next week except text Janey and thank her for the advice. "Elroy answered all my questions," he wrote, and it was true, the more he thought about it.

The following Tuesday, everyone seemed to be acting normal toward him, although he kept his distance from the basses, and David and Hal specifically. After the break, Dr. Simoneaux announced whom she'd chosen for the bass solo: Christina. The altos cheered while the basses clapped politely. Howard was relieved. Even though he'd already broken the Code, the stigma, he believed, was less likely to linger.

At the end of rehearsal, he caught up with David and Hal as they were walking out. He said, "Hey, guys...I just want to apologize. I didn't realize I was breaking the Code last week."

Hal and David looked at each other, then Hal spoke. "You *do* realize, of course, that if I chose to audition, I'd get *all* the solos."

Howard didn't know how to respond. David said, "My man is a pro."

Howard said, "Okay...you know what? I get it. I do. Thank you." He held up a hand. "It will never happen again, I swear."

David and Hal looked skeptical.

Howard dropped his hand. "Because the Code works for all of us."

David and Hal looked at each other. "I think he means it," said David.

"Time will tell," said Hal. ♪

Choraliers

"This is me you're talking to," said Vanessa. She was sitting in Claire's office at the high school.

Claire said, "I know." She sighed. "I don't know what else to say."

"How about, 'I'm putting Emma in Advanced Choir, because I know she has it in her, and the high-expectation environment will carry her to the next level.' Something like that would work."

Claire said, "I can't treat her differently because of our friendship."

Vanessa said, "I'm not asking for special treatment, I'm asking you to follow your gut and put the right person in your Advanced Choir. Actually, you'll miss her if you don't."

"I won't miss her, because she'll be a Choralier, which by the way is…"

Vanessa interrupted. "She won't stay in the Choraliers. As a senior? Are you kidding me?"

"I'm not kidding you," said Claire. "She has her friends there, and it's less…arduous."

"Are you saying my child doesn't want to work? I know you're not."

"No, no. I'm just saying she might prefer the culture of the Choraliers. Many students do."

Vanessa said, "She's gonna act like this is no big deal, but I know her. On the inside, it'll be tearing her apart."

"This is a part of being a singer," said Claire. "You know that."

"I suppose."

They were silent for ten seconds.

Vanessa said, "And you're one hundred percent sure Emma can't cut it?"

Claire said, "I don't like that language, but…yes, I'm sure she's not ready."

"I don't see how you can be so sure."

Claire said, "Do you sing with her much at home? Or does she let you listen to her practice?"

"No. Not since she got to high school. But that's normal."

Claire said, "And in her case, two singer parents, mom a professional…that casts a large shadow."

Vanessa said, "That's right! Think of how this child of two singers is going to feel when she finds out she didn't make Advanced Choir!"

"She's going to be fine," said Claire.

"There's still time to change your mind, isn't there? Can't you make a slot for her? I promise I will personally make sure she pulls her weight and more."

After a long pause, Claire said, "Emma doesn't have the skill set for a spot in Advanced Choir. I don't know how to say it any more plainly."

"She's going to be devastated," said Vanessa. "But you'll tell her in a nice way, right? Tell her the Choraliers are a better fit for her voice type, or it's a slower pace, or whatever...when in reality, Emma knows the truth, just like we all do: She's *not good enough* for Advanced Choir."

"I think that's what I just said," said Claire.

"Hmph. When are you going to tell her?"

"I post the rosters day after tomorrow."

Vanessa stood up. "Well, thank you for letting me know. I'm sorry for acting like a crazy person. This is hard for me."

Claire said, "I know. Emma's a happy kid, though, and she'll be happy wherever she is."

"I can tell you one place Emma *won't* be is the Choraliers. No chance." Vanessa went to the door. "Have a good day." She walked out and came right back in. "I appreciate your telling me, and I know you're doing what you think is right. Please reconsider, though, okay? For me?"

"I can't do that, I'm sorry," said Claire.

"Alright. I get it. Thanks anyway."

From the car, Vanessa called Kelly.[1]

"What's up?" said Kelly.

---

[1] Vanessa, Claire, and Kelly are professional singing colleagues.

"I can't believe it," said Vanessa. "Claire isn't putting Emma in Advanced Choir."

"Oh, no! Did you talk to her about it?"

"Talk to whom?"

"To Claire."

"Yeah, I just left the school," said Vanessa. "She won't budge. She says Emma doesn't have the talent. Basically."

"Oof. That's..."

"It's bullshit is what it is, and Claire knows it."

"What are you gonna do?" said Kelly.

"Well...Emma's going to resist, but I think we should look at some other schools. I don't know."

"That could be tough," said Kelly. "Senior year."

"And I have to spend the next two days pretending not to know, then act surprised when Emma tells me. I'm not looking forward to *that*."

"Let me know if I can help," said Kelly.

"I don't know how you can, but thanks."

On Friday, Vanessa had been expecting a teary call or text from Emma by early afternoon but had received nothing. Vanessa texted her around the time school let out, "just to say hi," but Emma didn't respond.

Vanessa got home at 5:30. Emma was in her bedroom with the door closed. Vanessa knocked. Emma opened the door. She looked spent. "Hi," she said. "Doing homework."

"How was your day?" said Vanessa.

"It was fine."

"Good. Let me know when you get hungry."

"Okay," said Emma. "I'm gonna close this, okay?" She held the knob. "I concentrate better."

"Sure, yeah. I'm lucky you're such a good student." Emma started closing the door. Vanessa said, "Wait...didn't you get your choir assignment today? For next year?"

Emma said, "We were supposed to, but Miss Collins needed more time. We'll know sometime next week."

"Next week?"

"Yeah, hopefully."

"Oh...that's weird."

"I guess," said Emma. "It's not a big deal, anyway. I keep telling you."

"Alright then...have a good...homework session."

"Thanks," Emma said, and closed the door.

Vanessa dialed Kelly. "What the hell?" said Vanessa. "The rosters were supposed to get posted today, but Emma says Claire put it off. I wonder if she's reconsidering."

"Maybe she is," said Kelly.

"Do you think I should call her? No, I won't. I've said too much already, probably, although if she's really reconsidering, maybe..."

Kelly said, "Hey, Vanessa, I gotta go, alright? Let me know."

"Yeah, I will, thanks."

By Sunday evening, Vanessa couldn't hold off any longer. She called Claire and got her voicemail. She left a message to please call her back, and it was *important*. Claire called a few minutes later.

"Hi Claire," said Vanessa. "Thanks for returning my call. I wasn't sure you would after our visit." She laughed but noted that Claire did not laugh with her.

Claire said, "Did she tell you?"

Vanessa said, "There's nothing to tell."

"What do you mean?" said Claire.

"I mean she told me that you held off on the rosters until next week, and…I was hoping it meant you were considering my request."

"What?" said Claire. "She didn't tell you?"

"Tell me what?" said Vanessa. "*What* is going on here?"

"The rosters went up Friday, and Emma's on the list for Advanced Choir."

"Really?"

"Yes."

"Wow! That is amazing! I don't know how to thank you! It's going to make such a difference in her life!"

Claire said, "So…what *did* she tell you?"

"Never mind that, she's just being a teenager. I'll get to the bottom of it, but…yay! Even if *she's* not thrilled, I'm thrilled enough for both of us."

"I'm glad to hear that," said Claire.

"So…can I ask…what made you change your mind?"

"Honestly, I got a phone call from Kelly, who helped me see the bigger picture. Or something like that. I don't know. I was always on the fence."

"You said Emma didn't have the talent."

"Yes," said Claire. "But ultimately, I decided I'm not ready to reach that conclusion. She's just a kid. And her genetics weigh heavily in her favor."

"Exactly!" said Vanessa. "Oh, the world feels right side up again! Thank you!"

"You're welcome," said Claire.

"Like I told you, Emma doesn't always let on how she's really feeling. Her dad says the same thing."

"High schoolers can be challenging."

"You would know!" said Vanessa.

After hanging up, a very cheerful Vanessa found Emma in the living room, watching television. She sat down with her and said, "Just so you know, I called my friend Claire—Miss Collins—to catch up, and she told me you made Advanced Choir! That's so wonderful!"

Emma smiled weakly but said nothing.

"Aren't you happy? And what's with this story you made up about next week?

Emma looked at her feet. "I didn't know how to tell you…I'm not joining Advanced Choir."

"What? Why not?"

Emma looked up. "I like the Choraliers. I want to stay there."

Vanessa was silent.

"See?" said Emma. "I knew this was how you'd react."

Vanessa shook her head. "No, no…I'm just…trying to understand."

Emma said, "I'm not great at singing, okay? But I like it, and I like my friends, and I like the Choraliers, and... that's all."

"First of all, you *are* great. You *are*. And the travel... the experiences...there's such a huge difference between Choraliers and Advanced."

"I know," said Emma. "It's like varsity and JV."

"That's a perfect way to put it," said Vanessa.

Emma said, "Didn't you know something was wrong when I didn't make Advanced Choir this year? Lots of juniors do."

"So you're a late bloomer," said Vanessa. "We have lots of those in our family. Look at your dad—he didn't even start singing until he was forty!"

"Maybe I should quit until I'm forty."

Vanessa shook her head. "Don't say that. You have a golden opportunity right in front of you! You'll get to go to Europe! I still remember my Advanced Choir trip to Australia. It was life-changing."

"Yeah. Europe does sound fun."

"You can always drop out if you don't like it and go back to the Choraliers. Would you be willing to do that? Give Advanced a try, at least?"

Emma waited a long time before answering. "Only if you make me."

"Oh, honey, I'm not going to make you. I'm trying to convince you...to make a good decision. A really big, important decision."

"I understand," said Emma. She turned off the TV. "I'm tired and I have school tomorrow."

Vanessa said, "It's all gonna turn out how it's supposed to, I promise."

They stood up and hugged. Emma said "Good night," and went toward her room.

"Good night," said Vanessa. "I'm proud of you."

Vanessa called her ex-husband, Theo. He answered right away. "I figured you'd be calling tonight," he said.

"Why'd you figure that?"

"Because by now you'll know that Emma's not joining Advanced Choir. After all these years of you talking about it."

"*Me* talking about it?" said Vanessa.

"Yeah, you," said Theo. "Since the day she was born, I swear."

"Well, I intend to convince her. I'm her mom and I need to help her make good decisions. Especially the big ones. This could affect her college applications, you know."

"You won't get any help from me," said Theo. "I want her to do what's right for *her*. Not what's right for you."

"Easy for you to say. You barely see her."

"Yet, somehow, I've known for months what you just found out. Good luck, Vanessa, and I'm hanging up." He hung up.

Vanessa stared at the phone. She dialed Claire again. Claire said, "I didn't do it for Emma. I did it for you."

Vanessa said, "For me? How's that?"

"Now you can tell yourself, and everyone else, that your daughter made Advanced Choir but opted not to join. You fill in the reason."

"Hold on...you *knew* she didn't want to be in Advanced Choir. You knew it last week when I was in your office."

"Yes," said Claire. "I've known for a long time, but it wasn't my place to tell you."

"And you put her on the roster knowing she'd decline."

"Yes."

"Which means...you didn't really reconsider, because she really *isn't* good enough for Advanced Choir."

"No, she isn't. Not yet, anyway."

"Uh-huh. Well...it'll give her a confidence boost, at least."

"Maybe," said Claire. "It feels disingenuous on some level, but...I'm doing the best I can."

"I just wish I wasn't the last person to know," said Vanessa.

"I don't know what to say about that," said Claire.

On her way to bed, Vanessa passed by Emma's room. She heard...singing?

She held a fist up to knock but didn't.

Instead, she put her ear to the door and listened. ♪

The Void

Janey opened her eyes. As her mind became awake and aware, the familiar sensation returned.

She looked at the clock. 3:15, shit. She'd slept for two and a half hours, and now she had to get up and get clear enough to work on her music before rehearsal. And the bills, hell. She was still sleepy, though. She rolled over, sinking deeper into the bed. She closed her eyes. The feeling in her stomach eased, ever so slightly.

4:05. Damn. And the void...

Her mother had suggested she get checked for an ulcer, which she did, and nope—this was garden-variety anxiety manifesting in a particular way. Janey sometimes wished it *was* an ulcer. Then, there might be a cure. Or a salve, at least.

She sat up and took a sip of water from the glass on her nightstand. She put her socked feet on the floor and stood. She thought about making the bed, but why? She'd be getting right back in it six hours later. Nobody would know, and if they did, would they care? (Her mom would.) She arranged the blankets and pillows. Good enough.

She looked down at herself, dressed in sweatpants and a T-shirt. She must reek of sleep. She'd have to bathe and change.

She looked at the clock again and calculated. Thirty minutes to go through and pay the bills. No, an hour. It was a big pile. 5:05. Fifteen minutes to shower and get ready, realistically. 5:20. And since rehearsal was a twenty-minute drive, and she'd volunteered to get there early to help set up the chairs (a decision she regretted), she'd need to leave by 6:00. Meaning she only had forty minutes to practice her music, which she hadn't been able to do all week. Well, hadn't been up to doing. Because of the void.

She decided to shower first. She'd be fresher and more awake when she sat down with the paperwork. She stood under the water, wishing it was hotter and there was more of it. She got out, dried off, put on a different pair of sweats, brushed her teeth, and swallowed a pill. Shit, she needed to eat something. Otherwise the med wouldn't work right, and she'd get the brain zapping that didn't hurt but was annoying as hell.

Her mental health had gotten markedly worse when her dad passed. His death wasn't unexpected—he'd battled cardiovascular disease for over a decade—but the hole it left in Janey's life was too big to fill with any SSRI. Like the hole in her midsection.

"It *will* get better," the therapist promised. Janey wanted to believe her, but what was the woman supposed to say? You're going to be anxious and depressed the rest of your life? From age twenty-seven on? Of course not. Janey's mother wouldn't keep paying a therapist who delivered such a message.

Not only did Janey miss her dad's willingness to make a joke out of anything (Theo from the chorus reminded her of him in this way), she missed the few hundred dollars per month that showed up in her checking account. Mom hadn't known, which was fine, but now Dad was gone, and Mom didn't believe in that kind of help. Money for therapy, yes. Money for health insurance and co-pays and prescriptions, yes. But helping to make ends meet? As in car payments, auto insurance, gasoline, groceries, rent, utilities, cellphone, internet? No way. Clothing and entertainment? When hell froze over. Mom was sure that once Janey figured things out financially, her mental state would improve. Step one, according to Mom, was getting a real job. Because the part-time proofreading gig was unreliable and had never earned enough to cover the necessities.

Janey sat down with the pile. There was a routine for this: Open everything and pull out the contents, then order the invoices in reverse by due date. So the oldest ones—or past due ones—got paid first. She threw away the envelopes and all the other crap that got mailed with bills these days and prepared her stack. Those were ready to pay. Next, she got online and gathered the bills from her email, putting them in the "Due" folder. Now came the tough part: seeing how many she could actually cover before the money ran out.

She glanced at the clock. It was already 5:20. Where had the time gone? She'd made progress on the bills, though, getting them ready. She could pay them later that night. Or the next day. Right now, she needed to look at her music.

She pulled up the email from Dr. Simoneaux that outlined, in typical Simoneaux detail, what they'd be rehearsing. Janey looked at the list, and her mood darkened. The Irish song, ugh. And not one Rutter piece, but two. Then there were the other foreign language numbers: German, French, Latin. But the Irish was worst of all. You literally had to write the words in your music phonetically, because how they sounded on the reference recording had nothing to do with the letters on the page.

She thought about giving up and going to rehearsal unprepared. She'd done it plenty of times, but it made rehearsal not fun, and she felt like she was letting everyone else down.

No. She would resist the temptation to stare at her phone, and instead get through as much music as she could. She pulled up the YouTube playlist on her tablet, put in earbuds, and began at the top.

She managed to get out of the apartment by 6:03, a little behind but close enough. From the car, she called Rochelle.

"Hello?" said Rochelle.

"Hey. You coming tonight?" said Janey.

"Yeah. Why wouldn't I?"

"I don't know. No reason."

After a pause, Rochelle said, "How are *you* doing?"

"Shit sandwiches, mostly."

"Sorry," said Rochelle. Another pause. "Anyway, I didn't practice at all this week, so it's gonna be a rough night for me."

Janey said, "I crammed just now, but I'm not where I should be."

"Yeah, me neither. Definitely not."

Janey walked in the door to find the chairs already arranged. Apparently, the eager beaver Daniel had gotten there earlier than usual and done it all himself. Good for him. (And she meant it—she was envious of his energy and cheeriness.)

The only person she could see herself talking to was Rochelle, who wasn't there yet, so she kept to herself, sitting down at the last possible moment. Not that she didn't like her neighbors—she did—but she and the feeling in her gut weren't in the mood for interaction.

After warmups, Dr. Simoneaux called for the Irish piece, as per the plan. The altos complained quietly to one other. Dr. Simoneaux asked Jackie to roll up the pitches. They did a full run-through, and it was *bad*. Dr. Simoneaux picked out the worst trouble spots, going over them by section. When it was the tenors' turn, Janey surprised herself with how well she sang. Those few minutes of practice had really made a difference. Dr. Simoneaux noticed, too. "Thank you, Janey, for working on this," she said. "The rest of you..." She shook her head and frowned.

Janey couldn't help but smile. Howard gave her a thumbs-up, mouthing a "Yeah!" Janey looked away, but the compliment, and the recognition, felt good. Not only that, she was starting to like the piece, despite its crazy phonetics and simplistic, folky melody.

The rest of rehearsal went accordingly: The pieces Janey had worked on she was able to sing better than expected. Not so for the two Rutters, which she'd skipped over at home, and which she'd force herself to get to during the upcoming week.

Janey got out quickly after rehearsal, buoyed by the music but not wanting to engage in put-away-the-chairs small talk. On the drive home, she caught herself humming the Irish tune. How did the last verse go, exactly? She pulled up the recording on her phone and played it through the car speakers. Oh yeah—that's how it was supposed to sound! What a gorgeous piece of music! Why hadn't she recognized this sooner? Having heard the thing a dozen times, and it being so obviously amazing.

She walked into her apartment invigorated. She put off the bills, because she wanted to work on the Irish piece while it was fresh in her ear, even though her voice must be tired from hours of singing. While she was at it, she went over both Rutters. Her dislike was reinforced, but she could feel herself getting a better handle on them as she labored.

It was almost eleven, but she still had energy. She paid the bills she could afford to, ate a snack of cut-up fruit, and got ready for bed. She was humming the Irish tune again. She hoped it would be on next week's rehearsal plan.

Lying in bed, she became aware: no void. How long had it been gone? Since the end of rehearsal?

No, earlier.

Maybe the therapist was right. ♪

Four Sopranos and an Elevator

It was the day of Dr. Simoneaux's first concert with the Repertory Singers. The board had decided to try a new venue, a Unitarian church, in hopes of realizing additional ticket sales to the large congregation. The chorus had been able to rehearse there only once, earlier that week, and the acoustics were good but not great. Another potential negative: The church was on the edge of town, leading some to worry their regular patrons wouldn't want to make the drive, especially with Dr. Tilton no longer at the podium.

Eleanor was the first singer to arrive. She saw Dr. Simoneaux going over her music in the front row of pews. "How are you?" said Eleanor. "Excited, I bet."

Dr. Simoneaux looked up. "I suppose I am. I just hope the choir isn't thrown off by the unfamiliar setting."

"That won't be a problem. You've worked us hard, and today's the day for it all to come together. I'm sure of it."

"Thanks for the vote of confidence," said Dr. Simoneaux.

Other singers filtered in, dressed in concert black. The earlier-than-usual call time had generated grumbles, particularly among the altos, but Dr. Simoneaux wanted the extra half hour to deal with any unforeseen complications.

After touching on the beginning and ending of each piece and going over the stage ingress and egress—always a challenge, for reasons no one understood—the group retired to the green room, directly behind the altar. Most of the singers sat in folding chairs arranged in a wide circle, but several members were left standing.

"You'd think they'd have enough seats for us," said Rochelle to Susannah. "If they want us back."

Susannah said, "I was sitting all morning, so I'm fine with it. My problem is with the size of this place. Even if we get a good crowd, it's going to feel empty."

"Whatever," said Rochelle. "We don't sound so hot anyway. I don't know if we've ever been this unprepared."

Marnie appeared from a hallway. "Hey sops, guess what I found? An *elevator*."

"What?" said Susannah. "Where did you go?"

"Just poking around," said Marnie.

Rochelle said, "I've never heard of a church with an elevator."

"It's not that uncommon," said Marnie. "But this one's weirdly hidden."

Susannah said, "There must be a basement." She looked at the high ceiling. "Doesn't seem like there's a second level."

"Maybe there's a secret floor," said Rochelle.

Marnie said, "We've still got twenty minutes before we have to line up. I say we check it out. See where it goes."

"Sounds fun," said Rochelle. "The mood in here is kind of a bummer anyway."

Susannah said, "Isn't Dr. Simoneaux gonna give a pre-show pep talk?"

Rochelle said, "She doesn't seem like the pep-talk type."

Marnie said, "It'll just take a minute. We won't miss anything."

"Let's do it," said Rochelle.

Susannah shrugged. "Alright."

Marnie beckoned with her folder and went back down the hall. Rochelle and Susannah followed with their folders. Susannah checked over her shoulder to make sure Dr. Simoneaux wasn't watching.

They came to a door with stenciled letters that read *Staff Only*. Marnie opened it. Susannah said, "We're obviously not supposed to go in there." She heard footsteps and turned to see Hazel approaching.

Hazel said, "What's going on back here? Am I missing something?"

Rochelle and Susannah frowned at each other. Marnie shook her head at both of them and said to Hazel, "We're checking out where the elevator goes. You can come if you want."

Hazel pointed. "But this says Staff Only."

Marnie said, "If it was that big a deal, they'd keep it locked."

"You'd think so," said Rochelle.

"It sounds naughty," said Hazel. "I'm in."

Susannah said, "I don't know…"

Rochelle said, "Come on, Susannah. We're just looking for the bathroom." She looked at Marnie. "Right, Marn?"

"Right," said Marnie.

Hazel said, "The bathrooms are by the…" She hesitated as the other three stared. "Oh, okay. I get it," she said, turning pink.

They went through the door, and Marnie led them down a narrower, dimly lit hall.

"It's creepy in here," said Hazel.

"Like a catacomb," said Susannah. "But we're not even underground."

"Not yet," said Marnie.

The elevator was at the end of the hall. Marnie said, "Here it is. And you know what's strange?" She pointed to the panel. "There's no marking on the button."

"That *is* strange," said Hazel. "How do we know if it goes up or down?"

"There's one way to find out," said Marnie. She pressed the button, and the doors opened.

"Like it's been waiting for us," said Rochelle.

"Right?" said Marnie. She stepped inside.

Rochelle and Hazel followed, but Susannah stayed out, putting a hand against the edge of the door to keep it from closing. "What's on the inside panel?" she said.

Marnie said, "There's only one button, and it's blank."

Hazel said, "Now we *have* to see where it goes."

Susannah said, "This doesn't seem like a good idea."

Rochelle said, "Come on, Sue. Be a soprano. Be bold." She laughed.

"Ooh, I like that," said Hazel. "I'm bold." She flexed an arm.

Susannah joined them wordlessly. Marnie pressed the button. The doors closed.

"Here we go," said Marnie.

Hazel said, "What if it goes to a dungeon or something?"

Rochelle said, "I seriously doubt it'll be that interesting."

Susannah looked up, then down. "Are we moving?"

"Doesn't feel like it," said Marnie. She pressed the button again. Nothing happened.

"What now?" said Rochelle.

Hazel said, "It seems like we're moving, doesn't it?" She raised up on her toes.

"We're definitely *not* moving," said Susannah. "We'd hear something."

They waited and listened. Marnie pushed the button a third time. Still nothing.

"This is not good," said Rochelle.

"What do you mean?" said Hazel.

Susannah said, "She means *not good*. Like we might be stuck in here."

"What?" said Hazel in a squawk.

"Whoa, whoa, there's no reason to panic," said Marnie. "I'm sure it's gonna..." She pressed the button three more times.

Rochelle pointed to a keyhole next to the button. "Maybe you need a key." She shook her head. "Uh-oh."

"Uh-oh?" said Hazel, with a worried look.

Susannah said, "There's no emergency call button. What the heck kind of elevator is this?"

Rochelle said, "It's not public, so it doesn't need the usual safety stuff, I guess."

"What are you talking about?" said Hazel. "Don't you need that stuff to get a license?"

Susannah said with an edge, "Do you see a license?" She turned all the way around. "I don't."

♪ ♪ ♪

Back in the green room, Dr. Simoneaux was addressing the singers. "Even if there were only *one person* out there, we'd still owe that person everything we've got. And not just musically, but..." She saw Eleanor's raised hand. "Yes? Eleanor?"

"Sorry to interrupt, but...we seem to be missing some sopranos. Four, by my count."

"I call that a good start," said Theo. He snickered, as did the altos.

"Not funny," said Eleanor. "Has anyone seen them? We're getting close to showtime."

Dr. Simoneaux said, "Could somebody please go find them?"

"I will," said Eleanor.

"Thank you," said Dr. Simoneaux. "They can't have gone far."

Eleanor left the room. Dr. Simoneaux said, "Now, as I was saying…"

♪ ♪ ♪

Of the four sopranos in the elevator, only two had their phones. Marnie was staring at hers. "I don't have service," she said.

Susannah said, "Me neither. Shit. And we're supposed to be lining up *right now*."

Rochelle said, "This is *bad*."

Hazel said, "Okay, okay. I need to breathe." She put a hand on Marnie's shoulder.

Marnie said, "What's wrong?"

"I get claustrophobic," said Hazel.

Rochelle said, "Then why the hell did you get in an elevator?"

Hazel said, "I didn't know it was gonna…" She took deep, slow breaths and closed her eyes.

Marnie said, "It's alright, Hazel. Just try and stay calm." She patted Hazel on the back. "I'm sure we'll get out soon."

"How?" said Susannah. "How are we gonna get out?" She banged on the door and yelled, "Help!" It was jarring in the small space. Hazel whimpered and slid down the wall into a sitting position.

Rochelle said, "Wait! That's...I bet if we all yell, they'll hear and come find us!"

"Don't yell," said Hazel from the floor. "Please." Her face was pale.

Susannah said "I *knew* this was a bad idea."

Marnie said, "Don't worry, Hazel, we're not gonna yell." She crouched down and put her face in front of Hazel's. "But you can sing an E6, right?"

Hazel blinked twice. "Yes. I can."

"Good," said Marnie. "Because we need you. It's gonna take all of us."

"Okay," said Hazel. "I can, I can..." She stood up with Marnie's help.

Marnie said, "On my signal, we sing our highest note. As loud as possible. Without screwing up our voices, I mean."

Susannah and Rochelle nodded. "Good thing we're warmed up," said Rochelle.

Marnie looked at Hazel, who'd closed her eyes. "Hazel? Are you still with us?"

"Yes," said Hazel. "I'm just...focusing." She opened her eyes, set her folder on the floor, and put her hands over her ears. "Ready."

"Good thinking," said Marnie. She set down her folder and put her hands over her ears, as did Rochelle and Susannah. The four of them faced one another.

♪ ♪ ♪

Eleanor thought she might've heard a thumping noise but wasn't sure, and she couldn't make out which direction it had come from. This new noise, however, was unmistakably soprano. The chorus and the audience must be hearing it too. She went toward it until she came to the *Staff Only* door. She pushed it open. The sound got much louder, then stopped. She saw the elevator at the end of the hall.

The noise started up again. From the elevator! She ran to it and pressed the button. The doors opened. The missing singers—eyes closed, hands over their ears—were blaring high notes. The soundwaves hit Eleanor like a passing train's, causing her to stagger back. The four sopranos opened their eyes and stopped singing.

"Thank God!" said Hazel. She picked up her folder and pushed past Susannah to exit the elevator. The other three filed out.

Eleanor said, "What in God's name were you doing?"

"We'll explain later," said Marnie. She looked at her phone. "Shoot, we gotta go."

"I'll say," said Eleanor. "The audience is waiting."

The wayward sopranos were red-faced as they took their places in the green room. Eleanor looked at the clock. "This is a first."

Marnie caught Hazel's eye and gave her a waist-high thumbs-up. Hazel responded with a prayer gesture and mouthed, *Thank you.*

Dr. Simoneaux, expressionless, prompted the chorus to enter the sanctuary. ♪

A Betrayal

Apart from starting ten minutes late, Dr. Simoneaux's first concert with the Repertory Singers went fine. Not great, fine. The two subsequent performances were better, but the quality was still not at the level audiences—and the singers themselves—had come to expect over the organization's long history. Making matters worse, attendance was down across the board, meaning the financial results of the spring cycle would turn out poorer than budgeted. In light of these realities, finger-pointing was to be expected.

Dr. Simoneaux sat down at her computer to go over the "Feedback for the Director" survey she'd sent to the choir the day after the last show. Surprisingly, forty-one of the forty-five singers had responded within a week. Was that a good sign? Or a bad one?

She opened the first tab and saw an email address at the top: KatieH2008@qmail.com. Huh? This was supposed to be anonymous. She should exit the program and get in touch with Daniel, who'd helped her set it up. But before she could move the mouse to close the window, her eyes drifted down the page. A sentence jumped off the screen: *The bell kind of makes me feel like I'm in kindergarten.*

She looked at the email address again. It had to be Katie Harrelson, the soprano who sat next to Eleanor. Easygoing, hardworking, and supportive, Katie was one of Dr. Simoneaux's favorite singers.

She kept reading. *I understand the value of the metronome, but the reality is, nobody likes it, and you should probably get rid of it.* And farther down: *The choir doesn't seem as unified as in the past.*

If this was what one of her supporters thought, what would the other responses be like?

But back to the email address. Could it be a one-time glitch in the software? No—when she opened the second tab, she saw another address: TJMcHenry@coaster.net. From the last name, it belonged to Theo, the wisecracking bass. She swallowed hard. She should stop right there and let Daniel know. He could get it figured out and send her the data without the addresses showing. Or put it in a different format. There'd be a number of ways to get around this, the only downside being she might have to wait another day or two before diving in.

Theo's words were right there on the screen. She couldn't resist. *You treat everyone with fairness and respect in my opinion, but your overall approach could use some adjustment. Please don't take this personally.*

If not personally, how was she supposed to take it?

There must be singers whose comments were more encouraging. Mustn't there? Eleanor, for example. Eleanor understood the concept of short-term pain for long-term gain. She'd said as much during their discussion over drinks. She'd even come around on the ensemble metronome work.

The answer was only a few clicks away. Dr. Simoneaux opened up each tab, checking the top line, until she saw Eleanor's address, which she'd memorized, because Eleanor hadn't been shy about communicating. She hesitated.

The singers had filled out the survey with an expectation of anonymity. Without anonymity, there could be no honesty. And without honesty, their feedback was of no value. But, as music director, it was *her* job to bring out the best in the group. So who were these members to tell her how to do that? They weren't even being paid to sing. Did Robert Shaw ask the Cleveland Orchestra Chorus for suggestions? Certainly not. Because Robert Shaw knew what he was doing and what he wanted to do. This group wasn't the COC, but an ensemble was an ensemble was an ensemble, and the music director was its leader. LEADER, in capital letters.

Something else nagged at her: how the singers crowded around Dr. Tilton when he attended the final performance. And how they'd tried to sing their very best *for him*—although it wasn't enough to overcome a collective lack of preparation. In truth, she hadn't even planned on doing a survey. Not after the first cycle, anyway, until she'd been encouraged to by...Eleanor. Eleanor had been insistent and persuasive that night at the Lazy Nickel.

She had to know. She looked at Eleanor's entry.

You treat this choir like a job instead of a family.

None of the singers like you.

In all my years, the choir has never sounded this bad.

You're not the right person to lead this group.

Eleanor had tricked her, pretending to be an ally. So much for soprano bond.

She could tell Daniel she hadn't looked at any of the senders, but would he believe her?

She'd come too far to stop now. She went back to the beginning and read through every response. She didn't even bother to look at the email addresses—they didn't matter at this point. While there were a few encouraging comments, most were along the lines of Theo's and Katie's. And Eleanor's.

She closed the program and opened the bottom desk drawer. Breaking her own rule, she poured a tumbler of whiskey from a bottle she kept for emergencies. Emergencies that would never come, until right now, when resignation seemed like her only option. She took a drink, opened her email, and selected "compose."

♪ ♪ ♪

Dr. Tilton was calling. She considered not picking up, but knowing him, and their history, he'd keep trying until she did.

"Hello, Armand."

"Diana, I heard the news! What in the world has happened?"

"They don't like me, Armand. And they should have a music director they not only like, but love. Someone like you."

"Well...why didn't you contact me sooner? I could have helped. In fact, I would've called to check on you had I any idea. I *should* have."

She was holding back tears. "I didn't want to disturb you. And I felt like I needed to walk on my own two feet."

He sighed. "I'm not going to argue with you, but... how about we get together in a few days, or a week, when things have settled down a bit? Could we plan on that?"

"Sure, Armand, I'd love to see you. But I'm certain of my decision."

♪ ♪ ♪

Four months later, the singers had arrived for the first rehearsal of the season. There were hugs and smiles and laughter, and the mood was altogether euphoric.

Dr. Tilton stepped onto the podium. The altos, including Mary Pat, quit jabbering when he clapped his hands.

"Choir, this is news to none of you at this point, but still, it gives me great pleasure to introduce your new interim music director, your erstwhile accompanist, Jackie!"

The singers cheered. Jackie stepped forward and took a bow. Dr. Tilton said, "I don't believe there's anyone on earth, including myself, who knows this choir the way she does. The strengths, the weaknesses, and everything in between." He waited for the applause to die down. "What you might *not* know is that she's been taking conducting workshops for the past several years, and I can tell you, she has all the skills she needs to be stellar on this podium."

Theo said, "Everyone hold on to your pencils!" and laughed. A handful of members laughed with him, while the rest looked at him quizzically. "Ask me about it at the break," he said.

Eleanor said, "As long as we don't have to sing to a metronome."

Janey said, "And no solfege, *please*."

David said, "No solfege? Come on!"

Dr. Tilton clapped twice. "Choir. You should also know that I'll be rejoining the group in a limited capacity, as a consultant." He pointed to no one in particular. "So be aware...I'll be watching. And listening." He looked around, stopping at Howard. "Is that our newest tenor I see?"

Howard raised his hand. "I'm Howard. Very glad to be here."

"I've heard so much about you," said Dr. Tilton. "Welcome!"

The altos snickered. Howard shook his head, and Janey put a hand on his shoulder.

Hazel said, "So who's going to be our accompanist?"

Dr. Tilton said, "We're still working on that. For this evening, it'll be yours truly."

There were delighted oohs and aahs. Dr. Tilton stepped off the podium, turning to Jackie. "And now, Jackie…are you ready to lead warmups?"

"I am, thank you," said Jackie. She sat down at the piano. "Let's start with…"

Janey was about to open her car door when she heard trotting footsteps. She turned to see Howard.

"Hey, Janey, you got a second?"

"Yeah," she said. "What's up?"

"You were super cool to me in there. Thanks for that."

"I'm not sure what you mean," she said.

"You know, when you…" He patted his own shoulder.

"Oh, right. Yeah. No worries. We tenors have to stick together. I used to be an alto, so…you know."

"Right, yeah." He paused. "Anyway, I was wondering if you'd ever want to hang out sometime, outside of here…the chorus, I mean, not the church." He gave a nervous laugh.

She said, "Are you asking me out on a date?"

"Yes," he said. "I am. I could take you out for a late dinner right now if…you have time. And you're hungry."

She looked down at herself. "I'm not really dressed for dinner."

He said, "I think you look amazing." He untucked his shirt and held his arms out. "See? Casual."

Janey looked over at Samuel and Mary Pat getting in their car across the lot, then back at Howard.

"Okay," she said. "Let's."

THE END

Encore

Emma and Theo

Saved for Last

Theo and his daughter were topping off their weekly Wednesday dinner at Bartleby's with hot fudge sundaes.

"Come again?" said Theo. He looked like he couldn't believe what he was hearing.

Emma laughed. "I said, I'm trying out for Regional Choir."

"Really. *That's* weird."

"I know what you think of competitive music."

"Yeah," he said, and harrumphed. "Your mom must be happy."

"I haven't told her yet. I wasn't planning to unless I make it. Then I'll surprise her."

Theo sighed and put down his spoon. "Could you please tell her now? It's awkward for me, you know, keeping secrets."

"The audition is Saturday," she said. "Can I wait until then?" Her expression was hopeful.

"Alright...but you need to tell her, even if you don't make it." Emma frowned. He said, "She'll be happy either way, because it means you've taken more of an interest in singing. Which is what she wants."

Emma said, "But if I *don't* make it, she'll be disappointed. I know her."

"Not as well as I do. Trust me, telling her is the smart thing to do."

Emma was silent.

Theo said, "Okay, fine, I'll leave it up to you. I don't want you not telling me stuff. Know what I mean?"

"I'll think about it," she said.

"Good, thank you." Theo took a bite and talked with his mouth full. "Things must be going well with the Choraliers." He held up his spoon. "Wait…so…Miss Collins, she must know. Right?"

"Yeah, Dad. She's keeping my secret because I asked her to."

"Your poor mom. The last to know, and the person who cares the most." Emma nodded. He said, "Not a coincidence, by the way." He took another bite.

Emma said, "I actually tried out for a solo last week and got it, so that's why I was thinking…I might have a shot at regionals. And Miss Collins is encouraging me, even though I'm not in Advanced."

"But you've been working on the music for a while, I assume. For the audition?"

"Yeah. I just didn't know if I was gonna go through with it."

Theo used his spoon to gather hot fudge that had overflowed from his parfait glass. "You'd have fun, anyway," he said. "Meet some new people."

"The wrong kind of people, you mean."

He laughed. "Yeah. The kind of people who do competitive music." He added quickly, "But if it turns out you're one of those people, I'll still like you."

"Thanks," she said. "The part I'm worried about is the sight-singing." She poked at her sundae.

"Oh, Jesus, sight-singing. Don't even get me started."

"You think it's bullshit, right?"

"Hey, watch your language," he said. "But, yes. Total bull."

"Could you tell me why again? Miss Collins and Mom and everybody else thinks it's a really big deal."

"Sure, I'll tell you why," he said. "Because sight-singing has as much to do with singing as competition has to do with art. That is, *nothing*."

Emma took a bite. "Keep going, please."

"Alright. Take me, for example. I'm a lousy sight-reader. My brain doesn't process fast enough. But in my choir, the Repertory Singers, which as you know is a darn good group, we work on the same music for three months. Got that? Three freaking months. So why the heck do I need to sight-read?" He pointed his spoon at her. "Tell me that."

Emma said, "There's an alto in Choraliers who's this, like, really amazing sight-singer, but she's not the best singer in the group. Not even close."

Theo nodded. "See what I mean? She probably only got into Choraliers because of her reading. I'm surprised they didn't put her in Advanced."

"She's really not good, Dad. Sorry to say. She's pitchy."

"Oof," he said. "There's no cure for that. But what do I know? I'm just an amateur."

"I think you sound good. When I've heard you."

"Thanks! Same to you."

They both laughed. Theo said, "You could ask the judges about it."

Emma widened her eyes. "They'd love that, I bet. Not."

"Heck, they actually might. You never know with judges. They're messed up to begin with. That's why they're involved with competitive music."

♪ ♪ ♪

Emma walked into her regionals audition very nervous. As Miss Collins had recommended, she focused on her breathing, keeping it slow and steady. But her heart was beating fast, and her hands were cold.

The adjudication assistant was a serious-looking older woman named Mrs. Bradley. She placed Emma's music on a stand and adjusted it to Emma's height before sitting down at the piano. Bisecting the room was a scrim, behind which must be the three judges. Emma rubbed her hands together.

They began with the vocalese portion, during which Emma had to sing scales and arpeggios along with the piano. No problem there.

Second came Emma's preprepared *a cappella* art song. She sang it with confidence and thought she performed as well as she could have under the circumstances.

Next was interval memory. Mrs. Bradley played short melodic passages that Emma had to repeat back in solfege. Emma did well with this, noting the passages were much simpler than what she'd prepared for. So far, so good. But as always with this type of audition, the worst was saved for last.

Mrs. Bradley handed Emma a sheet of music, gave her the starting tone and operative major scale, and told her she had one minute to prepare. *One minute*, thought Emma. In her head, she heard her dad saying *three freaking months*, and she couldn't help but laugh.

Mrs. Bradley frowned. "Is something funny?"

"No, no," said Emma. "Sorry." She bent her head down closer to the music, which she now had forty-five seconds to go over, but which suddenly looked like random black marks on a page. She took a deep breath and focused on the upper left. The key signature was...three sharps. A major. Or was it F-sharp minor? She could figure that out later. The time signature was 4/4. Okay, basic. The tempo marking was *andante*, or medium. The opening dynamic was *mezzo forte*, or medium loud. Everything about the piece seemed medium. Was that good or bad? Easy or some kind of trick? She looked at the melody. The first note was an A, so...

"Time," said Mrs. Bradley. She replayed the starting pitch and clapped the tempo.

Emma wished she hadn't laughed. She sang the first four measures, then...saw random black marks and stopped.

"Is something wrong?" said Mrs. Bradley.

Emma looked up. "I have a question." She said it loud enough that the judges would know it was for them. Mrs. Bradley frowned again.

After a long pause, a man's voice came from behind the scrim. "Go ahead."

Emma said, "You mean, go ahead and ask? Or..." She looked at Mrs. Bradley.

Mrs. Bradley said, "What is your question?"

"Okay..." Emma spoke to the scrim. "If I'm going to get the music for regional choir ahead of time...if I make it, I mean...why does it matter how well I can sight-sing?"

Mrs. Bradley shook her head. The voice said, "Sight-singing is an important indicator of overall musicianship."

Emma said, "But how? It seems like it's just an indicator of how *fast* I can apply my musicianship. If you know what I mean."

Mrs. Bradley looked at her wristwatch and stood up. "Your audition is over, Emma. We appreciate your participation. You'll be notified by email whether or not you've been accepted."

Emma held up a finger and looked toward the scrim. The voice stayed silent. Mrs. Bradley came over and picked up Emma's music off the stand, handing it back to her. "Thank you, Emma," she said. Her tone was unfriendly. She opened the door and held it.

Emma walked down the hall, tears welling up. She felt as if she were one inch tall. She got into her car and called her dad.

Theo couldn't understand what his daughter was saying, because of the crying. "What?" he said. "What happened? Are you alright?"

Emma gathered herself. "The audition was going good, really good, until the sight-singing." She cried again. Theo waited. "And then," she said, "I asked them. I asked the judges why sight-singing was so important...oh, they must think I'm such an idiot. I *feel* like an idiot."

Theo let out a long exhale. "Okay, wow. I guess...this is my fault. I mean, it *is* my fault. I am so sorry."

Emma was sniffling. Theo said, "I should keep my stupid mouth shut is what I should do. I'm the idiot. I gave you bad advice, and it's...yeah, I'm really, *really* sorry. I don't know what else to say."

"It's fine. I'm the one who opened my big mouth."

"No, no, I need to be a better father. That's what needs to happen," he said. "And I promise, I'm going to do that. In all ways."

"Okay. It's okay."

"Where are you?" he said. "Do you want me to come get you?"

"No, I'm fine. Thank you." She pulled a tissue from a box in the center console and blew her nose.

"Tell you what," he said. "Go home and tell your mom everything, including the part about me totally screwing this up. Okay? Then I'll wait for her to call me, or you two can call me together, and I'll apologize to both of you. Okay? I really feel bad. Horrible." His voice quivered.

"Maybe I will. Mom's gonna be pretty mad at you." She let out a little laugh.

Theo said, "In this case, she has a right to be. I'll take my medicine and like it." In a jokey voice he said, "Could I have some more please? Madam?"

Emma laughed fully and wiped her eyes. "I'm gonna hang up now. We'll talk later, I guess."

"Sweetie, I'm...really sorry, and I'll be waiting if you want to call."

"Okay, thanks. Bye." She hung up and headed home.

♪ ♪ ♪

Theo and Emma sat down in their usual booth the following Wednesday. Theo said, "Look, before you say anything, I just want you to know, I'm still so sorry, and the fact is, I say all kinds of bull you-know-what, but I don't know what I'm talking about. I'm a loudmouthed, know-it-all fool. But I can change."

Emma smiled. "You're not that bad, Dad. You make some pretty good points, actually."

"Yeah, well...you must've gotten your kindness and patience from your mom, because it didn't come from me."

Emma gave a slow nod, flaring her nostrils and lifting the corners of her mouth.

"What?" he said.

"I made regionals." Her face blossomed into a full grin.

"Really? That is freaking amazing! When did you find out?"

"Monday. But Mom and I decided I should wait to tell you in person."

Theo looked like he'd received the best news of his life. "I'm so happy for you, and relieved, and...that is *awesome*."

"Yeah, thanks. I was surprised, too."

Theo said, "So you're going, right? You said yes?"

"Yes. And I'm planning to try out for All-State."

"Cool!" he said. "Go for it!" He pumped a fist. "You can do it."

"Because I'm starting to think...competitive music might be my thing."

He nodded. "Well, I've changed *my* thinking, too. I don't need to be so black and white about it."

Emma slapped the table. "Sight-singing still sucks, though. I haven't changed my mind about *that*, even though I *will* get better at it."

Theo started to say something, but stopped. His hand went to his mouth with a zippering gesture.

Then, he picked up his menu and smiled. "How about today…we lead with dessert?" ♪

Acknowledgments

Thanks to Rebecca Salome, my writing coach and editor.
Thanks to book and cover designer Pia Zaverukha.
Thanks to beta readers/chorus consultants Cindy Johnson and Melissa Solyn.
Thanks to proofreader Nara Shin.

About the Author

Alejandro Canelos was born in Nogales, Sonora, and raised in Tucson. He studied biology at Harvard, receiving a B.A. in 1992. He is the author of three short story collections, two books of ten-minute plays, and a growing number of full-length plays. He also plays drums professionally (freelance, all styles) and sings in two choirs. In his spare time, he hikes, bikes, cheers on the UA Wildcats, and spends time with his family.

Made in the USA
Coppell, TX
27 February 2026